CADENCE OF THE Xylophone

ISBN-13: 978-1-961802-13-1

For everyone who lusted after the Phantom.
Oh, and if you've ever wanted a shitty man to die.

Author's Note

This is an erotic paranormal novella. It is mostly smut with a side of plot.

Trigger Warnings:
Attempted Murder/Murder
Blood
Torture
Death
Misogyny
Sexual Harassment
Slut Shaming
Stalking

Content Warnings:
Sexually Explicit Scenes
Mild BDSM Aspects
Adult Language
Mild Primal Play

Chapter One

Melody

Music lives in my soul, filling me up in a way no man ever has. It's my one true love. A life measured in notes and chords—the flowing cadences and uplifting crescendos followed by the crashing waves of melody.

Every time I play, whether it's in my tiny apartment on the east side or here in the orchestra pit, I'm more alive than before. It's the only path I've ever sought, and I can't imagine a world without my music.

Tonight is no different, except for the eyes that follow me. Chad hasn't been with our team long, but he's proclaimed himself the lead of our section. As if a timpani player could ever be in charge of a percussionist.

I may have gagged when he told me he was a "nice guy." Everyone avoids him, but since his timpani are next to me, I can't seem to shake him. Even now, when we're supposed to be warming up, he's paying more attention to me than to his music.

I run my finger along the wooden keys of my xylophone, and a thrill skitters up my spine. I love playing, but this particular instrument has been in the theatre for centuries. Lately, my dreams have been filled with the clear notes of this xylophone, which fill my veins with fire. I wake up hot and sweaty, pleasure pulsing through my body with every heartbeat. So far, I've managed to ignore the burning in my gut while I'm performing. Every night it gets harder and harder, though.

"Melody, dear," Chad calls over the sound of a dozen stringed instruments clashing with the high-pitched notes of the woodwind section.

I close my eyes, gripping my mallets with one hand and splaying the palm of my other on the bars. The coolness from the wood centers me enough to ground me to the present, giving me the strength to deal with him.

"Yes, Chad?" I keep my voice neutral, hoping to not encourage him any more than necessary.

Our eyes meet and I fight the urge to back away from the intensity in his dull brown eyes. His gaze darts down to my hand still touching the bars, and his lip curls. I don't know what his problem is with my instrument. If he comes any closer, I'm liable to shove my mallet down his throat and damn the consequences.

His face clears, a simpering smile plastering itself on his mouth. "Sorry, I'm always so caught by your eyes. They're such a brilliant blue. I swear I could drown in them if you let me."

My stomach turns as he scans me up and down. "Was there something you needed, Chad?"

"I noticed the way you hold your mallets is just a little loose. It might help to grip them a bit tighter. Then when you're stroking the keys, they'll sing for you in a way you've never heard before."

It takes everything in me not to throw up on his polished black wingtips. Instead, I throw my shoulders back and tip my chin up. When Chad asked me out the first time, I was gentle in my rejection. The next time he insinuated we'd make a great couple, I was firm but polite. I don't need to be fired from this job. As it is, I'm on the verge of losing my apartment. I thought Chad would give up when I made it clear I wasn't interested.

Except he's taken to handing out asinine compliments on my appearance, then criticizing the way I play. I can take a lot of things, but this is not one of them. Don't fuck with my passion.

"I don't need your advice, Chad. I've been playing for twenty years and have perfected my skills. Please go back to your own instrument. It's looking a bit underused."

He sniffs, rage flashing in his eyes, and I fear I've gone too far. Usually I thank him, placating him the best I can. He blinks and the anger vanishes as if I imagined it.

"Of course you're a...wonderful xylophone player, Melody. I'd never question your skills." His mouth twists, like we're not talking about my musical abilities at all. Gross.

A single note rings out, bright and clear, and peace steals into my bones. I can handle Chad and his disgustingness so long as we're interrupted by the start of another performance. I just wish he'd leave me the fuck alone, then this would be the perfect job.

Chad's eyes dart to the xylophone, confusion splashing across his face. He wanders away, like he couldn't remember why he came over in the first place.

I stopped questioning my instrument long ago. I've accepted that we have a special relationship, an understanding flowing between us. He, because I can't think of my xylophone as an 'it,' holds the memories of this theatre within its wood.

Does it make me a little unhinged to think I have a special connection to a piece of equipment most people wouldn't look at twice? Maybe. But other people don't have to understand it. I'm not about to tell anyone about it, though. X and I are cut from the same cloth...or rather the same wood? I shake my head, giving up on the metaphor.

The lights overhead dim once, twice, three times, and the patrons take their seats. Tonight is the final performance, and the theatre is packed. Bright lights obscure their faces, transforming them into a blur of nothingness that allows me to fall into the music with ease.

Chad's persistence fades away. My worries about affording my next rent payment disappear. The lack of a partner to share my life with vanishes until all that remains is me and my xylophone. I'd give anything to live in this moment forever.

Chapter Two

Xavier

For years I've been trapped, waiting for the one who would wake me up in more ways than one. And now that she's here, I'm still stuck within this instrument. The xylophone was lucky to escape the fire all those centuries ago. As I knelt in the ashes covering my once grand theatre, I cursed the pristine piece. Two hundred years later and I'm still cursing this wretched thing. They may have rebuilt my legacy and left the xylophone in its rightful place, but no one ever knew what happened to the owner.

Being encased in wood and metal, no one heard my pleas for salvation. No one cared what occurred or who had set the fire upon my beautiful building. They merely went on with their day, living their lives until they died while I remained, harboring bitterness deep within my nonexistent heart.

Melody is the one bright spot in my existence. Others before have played my keys, some rougher than others. None of them have elicited the exquisite refrains she has. It wasn't until she arrived that I realized how much control I had over the sounds flowing from the xylophone.

We work in harmony, creating euphoric compositions. Sometimes I feel as if I can reach out and touch her. Instead, I'm left to wait for the lingering stroke of her soft fingers, the occasional brush of her arm, the rare kiss of her cheek.

My bars vibrate with every strike of her mallet. This particular composition was always my favorite, with the rise and fall of a story wrapped around the notes. I enjoy the lilt of the flutes weaving with the strings, only to crash into the brass section. But the clear chords Melody extracts from me are like nothing else I've heard before. I've long raged against the curse confining me in this instrument. I don't mind it so much when Melody plays.

As the song slows, sending whispers into the crowd, a boom echoes above the rest. It's probably not as loud as I imagine, but since they've placed the xylophone right next to the timpani, the sound rattles my keys.

Fucking Chad.

Melody holds the same sentiment as me, based on the pained expression gracing her heart-shaped face. Her plump lips purse as she refrains from cussing him out. How I'm able to see them is unknown. I didn't use to be able to smell, to see, to feel—not until my intoxicating little muse entered my world.

I'm not always confined to the xylophone, yet the life I live as a phantom within these walls isn't enough. One day my little angel of music will walk these hallowed halls with me. We'll create our own symphony to rival any that's come before.

Chad's eyes track my Melody as she plays a particularly tricky combination, her eyes fixed on the sheet music sitting just behind me on a stand. Her pink tongue slips between her teeth, and I groan internally. I'd never interrupt her while she's playing, but the intensity within her captivating eyes calls me to. I wonder what it'd be like to ravish her on top of this xylophone.

The song comes to a close, and Melody gazes upon me as if she knows I'm stuck within this void. Can she feel me here, silently supporting her the only way I'm able? Probably not, though I've spent long enough encased within this instrument to know her emotions. She despises Chad, tolerates everyone else, and loves music. Perhaps it would be too much to assume she would be as enchanted by me as I am with her.

The stroke of her fingers along my bar shakes me from my pensiveness. I've adopted the language of this time quite well for someone who doesn't speak to another soul, even when I've temporarily broken free from my prison. Sometimes I slip into my past unconsciously.

I spend the rest of the performance basking in the glow Melody creates. It's as if the sun shines around her, creating a halo of beauty that can't compete with her. The sun pales in comparison to her and the music she creates. I keep waiting for the moment she'll disappear—taken from me before I'm ready to release her. If I could chain her to this place, share my curse just enough to confine her to my theatre, I fear I would.

This world is different from the one I lived in. Women are no longer relegated to the household, though from the way Chad treats Melody, apparently some of those tendencies have hung on. I'd love to say I never shared the beliefs of my fellow aristocrats, however, I was terribly pretentious in my youth. I suspect it's part of the reason I was cursed in the first place.

If I were free...I would no longer know how to act. I would never survive within the ranks of men like Chad. I shudder at the thought of such a thing. No, I'm much better ensconced within my theatre, even though I miss the freedom of walking amongst others. Or witnessing the final gasps of daylight streaking across the sky. Both of those experiences would never compare to Melody, though. I'd gladly live a thousand lives trapped in the dark if only for a glimpse of her in the throes of ecstasy.

A soft smile graces her plush lips as she gazes down at me, her mallets preparing for the finale. I brace myself for the end, knowing this is the last performance for now. She'll leave for a few weeks while I wallow, reliving the memories of her playing so passionately. She's the only reason I haven't fallen into despair. I brush the thoughts from my mind, determined to relish these final moments together.

Chapter Three

Melody

Two hours later, the last note rings into the silence, my chin trembling with the vibration from my xylophone. I've been here for over a year and I swear he's never sounded so clear, so strong, so enchanting. I shudder, my body curling over the bars as I cling to some semblance of normalcy.

Being turned on by music probably isn't all that wild. This is more than that, though. My desire seems directly tied to X. Perhaps I should stop imagining him as a *him*. It's bad enough I named him. He's...*It's* just an instrument. Nothing more, nothing less. Sure he's...*it's* a masterpiece—a piece of history left within these hallowed halls. That doesn't mean he...*it* should be confused with a living, breathing person...thing...whatever. My problem lies solely in the fact that, for me, music is life. My heart would cease to beat without the tempo of a song to guide it through this wretched world.

I press my cheek to the bars, the vibrations still resonating through me. I'll deal with my obsession and my body's strange reactions to a xylophone tomorrow. Tonight is for us—the final night of a performance. Before I know it, I'll be back, practicing a new piece, a new play, a new set of chords. It can't come soon enough. I'm already mourning the time I'll be off.

Chad clears his throat and I straighten. Rage coils through me at the interruption. I school my face into one of neutrality before facing him. He gives me a withering look, then sidles closer, invading my space in the process. I turn, resting my ass on my xylophone. Truthfully, I don't think he'd attack my instrument. I'm not taking any chances, though.

"Are you injured?" he asks, scanning me up and down.

I glance at my white button-up shirt that's no longer crisp. Ugh, I'm covered in sweat. Taking off my bra will be an amazing experience tonight. I wish I could whip it off right now, leaving my shirt draped over the instrument currently holding me up. Until Chad steps even closer, then places his hand on X. The last thing I want to do is be anywhere close to naked in front of him.

I stare at his dirty fingers, unable to get past the offense. "I'm fine. Please remove your hand."

He doesn't do as I ask, instead using his other hand to brush a strand of hair that's escaped my ponytail behind my ear. Fear slices through me, my gut flipping as his cologne infiltrates my senses. He runs his nose along my jaw. In another situation, with another man, it might be sexy. With Chad, it only serves to make me want to puke all over him.

"You need to stop running from me, Melody. The chase was fun for a while, but I'm growing tired of your feigned resistance," Chad whispers, his hot breath in my ear making me cringe.

I'm trapped between X and Chad, desperately wishing someone else would come along. Unfortunately, this area is set away from the others for some reason. Half the players are packing up, the rest congregating near our conductor. Patrons filter out of the theatre, creating the perfect cover for Chad's advances.

"I'm not playing hard to get, Chad. I'm not interested." I try to say it forcefully, but my voice wavers and he grins.

"Let's pack up and I can bring you home." He eases back the slightest bit, but not enough.

"I don't need a ride. Besides, I have plans." I don't. He doesn't need to know that, though.

He chuckles, retreating to collect his music. "We both know that's not true. And don't worry about putting me out. You'll be the only one putting out tonight. Plus, your place is on the way to mine. We can even go to that cute diner you seem to love so much beforehand."

My lungs seize as another flash of fear hits me. He knows where I live. He knows my plans. How long has he been following me? Tracking my movements without my knowledge? A shiver rolls down my spine at the thought of him spying on me. No, not spying—stalking. He's been tracking me, playing a game I didn't even know I was a contestant in. I swallow hard, unwilling to close my eyes. Not when Chad keeps glancing at me.

I step away from X, my body protesting the loss of security I felt just seconds before. I gather up my music and tuck it in my bag, then grab my mallets and shove them inside.

Usually, I'd take my time, basking in the glow of another performance well played—relishing my time wiping X down and cleaning my mallets. Not tonight. With Chad's thinly veiled threats hanging over me, the need to flee overwhelms me.

"Running will only excite me more, little bunny," Chad murmurs.

Blech. What a terrible nickname to give someone you don't know. The heat from his body seeps into my back, and I break out in a cold sweat.

A clear tone rings out, wrapping around me and warming me from the inside out. A peace steals over me, sending a rush of desire through my body. Between the threat at my back and the serenity swirling from the front, I'm suddenly lightheaded.

Slowly, I ease away from Chad, then spin to face him. With each step my muscles relax. Perhaps it's the distance, but more likely it's my hand resting on my xylophone. I always thought it was my increased confidence as I played more. Now I'm thinking it's because of my reliance on my xylophone. He...*It*...aw, hell— He gives me more strength than I'd ever gather on my own.

"Leave me alone, Chad. I'm not going anywhere with you. If you don't—"

"You'll what? Talk to the director? Or perhaps the police? No one would believe you. They never do." Chad smirks, then sweeps past me.

A chill rolls down my spine and I find myself frozen. I can't even blink away the terror rolling through me. He's done this before. I'm not his first victim. This isn't some ploy. He won't laugh and tell me he was joking. He's stalking me. Who knows what he'll do once he gets tired of chasing me. I don't want to find out.

His hot breath on the back of my neck jolts me out of my paralysis.

"I'll be waiting," he whispers.

I spin, tracking his movements as he saunters away. He doesn't bother to look back, confident in his ability to control me through fear. Asshole.

Leaning on my xylophone, I pull in deep breaths to calm my racing heart. "What am I going to do, X?"

Chapter Four

Xavier

I thought if I strained enough, I could transform before Melody left. Apparently, using the small amount of magic to distract Chad drained me. The rage I felt at him threatening her has dulled to a slow simmer.

If Melody would have stayed, then Chad might have come back for her, and I could have dealt with him. Instead, she spent time cleaning her space and the xylophone. I couldn't even enjoy her touch, I was so upset.

Now the curse twists out of me, magic swirling through the air before spearing into the xylophone. I black out briefly, floating through a void of nothingness. Time warps, sending swirls of light that morph into melodies until I'm standing upright in the attic of the theatre, blinking the spots from my vision. I stretch, my muscles protesting as I do so. Even after all these years, I'm never fully prepared for the transition between instrument to man.

I crack my neck, then set about finding garments. The modern clothes I've found left behind in the dressing rooms from past plays don't fit well, save one suit. They're better than nothing, which is exactly what I have since my entire wardrobe from long ago burned up in the fire. Or was lost to time. I spent a great many years while they rebuilt the theatre not being able to transform into an actual human. The only cherished possession I have now is Melody, and I don't truly own her. Not as I'd like.

And I may never have the chance. Rage rolls through me as I remember Chad's lascivious stare. A vicious grin forms on my face when I wonder if he'll search for Melody here. She's smart and therefore won't go home, knowing Chad will likely follow her.

If he comes looking for her at the theatre, he'll encounter a fate worse than death. There were secrets in these walls and buried in the floors even the fire couldn't burn away. And I know every single one of them.

Perhaps Chad would enjoy the catacombs hidden below the orchestra pit. Or the long-forgotten passageways weaving their way beyond the walls. Their design was a stroke of genius, if I do say so myself. Many said I went too far with them, what with the sudden drop-offs and mirrored dead ends.

I sigh, wondering if I was ahead of my time or merely the only one who understood the intellect behind such things. Melody would approve. She'd delight in the whimsy. My cock hardens as I imagine chasing her through the tunnels, her harsh breath leading me to her location. Her screams of pleasure would fill the space, echoing through the air and into my soul. After I gained her trust, of course. The image appears before me, then disappears just as quickly in a puff of smoke, leaving me bereft with my cock straining against my pants.

"I have to get out," I grunt as I prowl around my bed and toward the stairs.

The sooner I break this curse, the better. Not for myself, but for Melody. She deserves to live without the fear of a man. Especially a man like Chad.

The stairs creak as I descend, skipping the ones more rotted than the others. Replacing them has been on my list of things to do for a while, though I don't have nearly enough time while I'm corporeal.

I spent years, decades really, taking my rage out on whatever I could get my hands on. Several more were spent attempting to escape the sanctuary that has become my prison. Now, I make lists, slowly repairing my theatre. The current owners aren't aware of half the affairs they're neglecting. I'm sure it would help if they knew of the secret passageways, but that's neither here nor there.

If I was still in charge, nothing would be missed. Alas, that's not possible. At least not until I'm able to keep my physical body for longer than a single night.

I reach the orchestra pit, giving the xylophone a wide berth. I no longer resent the instrument, especially since it brought me Melody, but I still am not comfortable tempting fate. At any moment I expect to be sucked back into that blasted thing for another indeterminate amount of time. Melody may make the time go faster and the hours more enjoyable. Doesn't mean I relish my sentence within that void.

As soon as I breach the doors to the foyer, time slows. It's as if I'm walking through a dream, desperately attempting to reach a precious item. Yet the closer I get, the farther away it seems to be. I'll never reach that elusive freedom I've been striving for all these years. It was frustrating before. Now it's torture. With Melody lost to the outside world, there's nothing I can do to save her.

My limbs tremble as I pivot and prowl back through the doors. They thud shut behind me, echoing through my body like a death toll. Not that I'm able to die, but I imagine it's much like the emptiness I've experienced for decades now. The emotions which coursed through me mere hours ago are dissipating, leaving me bereft.

Shaking my head, I attempt to dispel the heavy thoughts from my mind. I doubt I'll accomplish any of the tasks I wanted tonight. Not with my focus on Melody and whether Chad has found her.

I stalk through the aisles, my lip curling at the hideous fabric they used on the seats. They should have gone with a classic color instead of this horrendous cream. They'll be replacing it within months. Humans are disgusting creatures regardless of whether they're allowed food and drink while seated.

I make my way backstage, checking the dressing rooms along the way. They're all empty, of course. No one stays long after a final performance. Some of the performers have parties, though I assume their soirées are vastly different from the ones I attended. From what I've overheard while trapped within that blasted instrument, they seem to be much tamer than the debauchery I engaged in. Wistful memories flit through my mind as I think back on those times.

As I approach the greenroom, I slow. A scuffling sound filters from behind the wood and I stop, pressing my ear against the door. Someone sniffles, their tears evident. Hope soars within my chest and I squash it. It's probably a new performer who fucked up their piece and decided hiding out was better than facing the others. Most of them don't last in an upscale place such as my theatre.

However, I've never run into anyone before. For many years I sequestered myself in my attic, then stuck to the tunnels for several more decades. Keeping within the shadows and away from others was the only way I kept my sanity in check. Now I wonder if I fucked up. Perhaps interaction was something that could have freed me from the curse.

My nose wrinkles at the thought. The only person I'd like to interact with is Melody. I'd rather whoever is holed up in the room leave. I have more pressing matters to attend to than comforting them. I wouldn't know how to do such a thing regardless.

I tip my head back, pulling in a deep breath, then knock softly. Perhaps I can strike enough terror in them at being caught in the theatre after hours that they'll be forced to flee. I have enough on my mind without worrying about someone else coming to investigate the noises they're bound to hear.

The sniffling stops as if they've frozen in place. Stepping back, I clasp my hands behind my back and wait for them to emerge.

No one calls out or moves, and my frustration grows. It rages out of control when another door quietly opens within the greenroom, and I heave out a sharp breath. They're trying to sneak away through the other exit, which only adds more work for me. Now I must waste time tracking them down to make sure they actually exit the theatre.

The heels of my boots click against the hardwood floors, and I contemplate taking them off. I'd rather not stalk someone in these ridiculous socks, though. They were hard enough to get used to, especially considering someone else wore them first. Nothing about this century makes sense and I've given up trying.

Soft footfalls echo through the hallway ahead, traveling deeper into the theatre instead of toward the front. Perhaps they assume they'll be able to slip out the back. Those doors are locked from the inside as well as out. I'll end up chasing them throughout the entire building, herding them away from my space.

A cruel smirk twists my lips when they slam into the blocked door and let out a muttered curse. Perhaps this won't be such a fruitless endeavor after all. It's been a long time since I've been able to terrorize someone. Engaging in such a pastime might take my mind off Melody.

Slipping a dagger from the sheath at my waist, gratitude for my habits from another time hits me. I've always worn a knife and that hasn't changed over the decades of solitude. I fight the thrill coursing through my body. No use getting worked up if it's someone not deserving of my antics. Scraping the blade along the wall might be enough to terrorize them, but it won't be sufficient for me.

I step around the corner and freeze as my eyes widen at the sight of Melody desperately attempting to gain access to the outside. My knife slips from my grip, and I scramble to keep hold of the blade. I shake myself from my stupor, then lean against the wall and observe her. Even a frantic mess, she's mesmerizing. Utterly enchanting, really.

While I'd hoped we'd meet someday, I never thought this particular wish would come true. My gaze travels her form, taking in her dark hair curling around her tear-stained face to her heaving chest, then the slope of her waist to the curve of her hips. Even her ankles are shapely, sending fire through my veins only to gather in my cock. She rears back her foot and kicks at the heavy wood, vexation washing over her features when the bar doesn't give no matter how hard she tries.

I clear my throat and she freezes, then turns wide blue eyes to me. I swear I could drown in the depths found within them. And I'd thank the waves for crashing into me and bless the current for pulling me under. Then I could reside inside her forever. Anything would be better than being trapped in the xylophone, but it would be a great boon to have her consume me with her gaze.

Her mouth parts as her eyes sweep over my frame. When her tongue darts out, running along her plump bottom lip, my cock strains against my pants. Desire washes over her heart-shaped face before she reins in the pleasure flowing through her body.

When her gaze returns to my face, I raise a single eyebrow and smirk. I imagined this scenario a thousand times before. I composed the notes that would make up our meeting, a lilting number filled with passion and carnal need.

Now that we're face to face, the moment is a series of rests I have to wade through before we can mold a masterpiece. My instincts take over, showing her the cocky asshole I am deep inside. She might as well know what she's getting into. Not that she has a choice. We are destined, regardless of whether or not she knows it.

Her tears dry up and she sways toward me. Perhaps it won't be so hard to convince her she belongs to me after all. The pull between us is too much to resist.

"Hello, little muse."

Chapter Five

Melody

Instead of demanding who the man standing in front of me is, a sigh leaves me. It's as if he's stolen the words from me and left me without a voice. Vibrations thrum between us, linking our souls together with a mystical thread. My muscles, so tight before, ease. And my mind slows from its frantic race to escape. Familiarity burns through me, and I narrow my eyes. I can't quite place where I know this man from, but I do. It resides within my bones, resonating through my body.

His suit speaks to another time period, clinging to his frame in all the right places. From the taper of his waist, I wouldn't be surprised if his crisp white shirt hides rock-hard abs and a delicious dip running along his hips.

Biting my tongue, I attempt to rein in the desire raging through me. There's something about him threatening to make me burst into flames. I shake my head, chalking it up to his strong jawline or the mystery swirling in his dark eyes. I've seen plenty of hot guys before. I won't come undone with one smirk of his gorgeous lips. No, not gorgeous—sensual. That's the type of look he's shooting me right now. These feelings flowing through me are nothing more than the fact I haven't been properly fucked in... a while. Unless I count my favorite toy. Which I don't.

I clear my throat, trying to find the terror I felt moments before. Usually, I wouldn't want to be afraid, but it might unlock my muscles enough to question him instead of staring at him like a lovesick fool.

"Cat got your tongue?" He smirks again, and I wonder if that's his signature move. I'm sure there's a massive line of women who have melted at his feet with that gesture alone.

"Do I know you?" I whisper, tilting my head.

He tucks his chin to his chest, but not before I catch his lips pulling into a full grin. Bastard probably thinks I've been watching him, just waiting for a moment like this to make my move.

His hand flutters at his side and my eyes widen when I spot the handle of a knife right before his coat settles back into place. I should be concerned about what he planned on doing with the blade before he found me. Instead, a thrill flashes through my body. Shit on a stick, I may be more fucked up than I thought. Or he has magical powers to override any fear cropping up within me.

When he crosses his arms, muscles straining against his shirt, I almost groan out loud. Thankfully, my survival instincts kick in and I swallow the sound along with the drool threatening to dribble down my chin.

Get your shit together, Melody.

My inner pep talk does nothing since he chooses that exact moment to lift his head and glance at me with hooded eyes.

Bad Melody. He's probably a serial killer. Who broke into an empty theatre. To set a trap for some unsuspecting soul. Or something.

"How long are you going to try to work out who I am, hmm?" His deep voice rolls through the air between us, filling my gut with warmth.

I tip my chin up, feigning confidence. "As long as it takes."

"That sounds more like a question than an answer, Melody." His jaw twitches as I stumble back a step.

"How do you know my name?"

He shakes his head, pulling an old watch from his pocket and the chain clinks against the metal. It pops open and he sighs before snapping it shut. It should make him look like a conductor confirming the train is on time. Instead, he seems sophisticated, as if he's from another world.

"We don't have much time, and I doubt I'd be able to explain it to you properly." The lilt of his voice is a balm to my soul after the roller coaster Chad put me through earlier. "However, we have pressing matters to attend to."

My mind zones out, latching onto the threat of Chad. His harassment is the reason I stayed in the theatre after everyone else was long gone. I didn't think anyone else would be here. I assumed everyone was off celebrating. They wouldn't care about the xylophone player who never mingled with them. Avoiding Chad was my only goal and now I'm standing in front of a six-foot-something tall drink of water and my lady bits are suddenly very fucking thirsty.

"*We* don't have any matters. I don't even know you." The breathlessness in my voice doesn't lend the confidence I want to show.

He pushes from the wall and saunters toward me. No—he's prowling. A shiver runs through me in anticipation. I shuffle away until my back hits the door. His hands land on either side of my head, caging me in.

As I gaze up at him with wide eyes, a sense of familiarity comes over me. I'm confident I've never seen this man before, but he strikes a chord within me.

He leans down and he pulls in a deep breath. "You smell divine."

He buries his nose into my neck and my head tilts, giving him more access. His lips brush against my skin as his fingers tug my hair band off, sending the strands cascading around my shoulders. He straightens, dark eyes dripping with lust, and he smirks yet again.

"We're going to have so much fun," he murmurs.

He grabs my hand and yanks me back the way he came. We pass the greenroom before I have enough sense to jerk away. I expect him to keep yanking me forward. Instead, he tightens his hold and stops, raising an eyebrow at me.

"Who are you?" I bite my cheek as my stomach flips.

A seductive smile overtakes his face. "Xavier Sebastian Cantrell the Third."

My mouth drops open as he drops my fingers and sweeps into a low bow. This man is not normal—at least not for this time period. I'd assume he was a cosplayer, but his mannerisms are too polished. His speech is too formal. Everything about this man screams he's from another world, stuck in ours for whatever reason.

"Uh, okay then. As lovely as this has been, I should get going."

I *should* walk away. Hell, I should run as far away from him as possible. He's got a fucking knife. Who knows what he'll do with it? He could be planning my murder. He'll stuff me in the walls and my ghost will haunt this place for eons. I *really* don't want to haunt an old theatre. Not by myself, anyway. Loneliness would eat away at me, and then I'd end up floating around listlessly.

I'm spiraling. That's the only explanation. I need to get out of here—preferably with my limbs still attached to my body. I pivot, ready to march toward the exit, then freeze when I realize the back doors will still be locked.

"And what exactly do you plan to do about Chad?" Xavier spits out the other man's name like a curse.

Slowly, I spin to face him. "What do you know about Chad?"

"I know he's a prick. I believe that's the correct word. I also know that he has nefarious intentions when it comes to you. And that you are in danger, which is why you were content to hide in the greenroom for however long in hopes that he would not be at your residence when you finally emerged." He straightens his cuffs, then peers at me.

"H-how...how did you know that?"

He shrugs, glancing away. "I listen. Not hard to decipher his schemes when he was practically shouting them in the percussion section."

"Chad and I are the only ones in that area of the section, though." My breath catches in my throat.

Alarm flickers in his eyes as he reaches for me. "I mean you no harm, Melody. I detest men like him. A woman should be willing —eager, if you will—to be chased. Otherwise, a man should find another partner to fulfill his fantasies."

I shake my head, trying to dispel the music dancing in my head. "That doesn't explain how you knew..."

A pulsing bass fills my ears—a drum reverberating through my body to a steady beat. Xavier is saying something, but all I hear are the layers of chords stacking on top of one another. It's as if there's a symphony within me, filling my soul with sweet dulcet tones. Xavier clears his throat, and the music cuts off.

His fingers trail down my arm, and I track the goosebumps he leaves in his wake. When he reaches my wrist, I jerk away. My mind bounces between my attraction to him and the fear of Chad coming for me.

Even if I hide here tonight, what happens tomorrow? And the next day? And the next? I'll never be free of him. Going to the police won't help since Chad hasn't physically hurt me. I could talk to the manager, but he's a pompous ass who didn't want to hire me in the first place. The director doesn't have that type of pull, either.

I bite my cheek as I take another step back, and he follows. "I don't know you."

"Don't you?" His thumb caresses my bottom lip. "Do you not feel the swell of intimacy? Or the ease with which your body responds to me? Do you not hear our song dancing along the wind?"

I swallow hard, lulled by his deep voice. Perhaps he's right. Maybe we have crossed paths and I merely don't remember. In another life, maybe we were something more than strangers trapped in an old theatre. Snapping from the spell he's put me under, I suck in a deep breath.

"I don't know what you're talking about," I gasp, even as my legs refuse to move.

He tucks a strand of hair behind my ear, then cups my cheek. "Oh, my delicious vision. How long will you fight this?"

"Fight what?"

"This bond between us. You feel it every time you play—the vibrations rolling through your body." He presses his body to mine and slips his arm around my waist. "The wetness gathering between your legs as that final note rings through the air."

I shudder, ducking my head into his chest. His fingers slide into my hair and my eyes fall closed. Gripping the strands, he tugs, tipping my chin up. His teeth graze my jaw and I swear my heart skips a beat. I didn't think that was possible, yet here we are.

My body doesn't care who he is. Or how he knows what I was feeling earlier while playing. Nothing matters but the pleasure thrumming through me. Pleasure he's creating.

He nips at my bottom lip, and his tongue darts out to soothe the small bit of pain. "Give into me. Show me how much you belong to me."

"B-belong to you? I-I don't belong to anyone," I stutter out while the rest of me tries to convince my mind to give in.

He snorts out a laugh, his breath ghosting across my ear. "You don't believe that. Your body doesn't lie, Melody. You *want* to belong to me, even if it's only for a night."

"Only for a night," I breathe.

I want to give in. I don't understand why, but I do. It's been too long since someone has wanted me. Maybe it's merely my libido bursting onto the scene.

One night wouldn't be so bad. I'd be safe from Chad and have a fun-filled time with a handsome stranger. People do this all the time. I've never had the pleasure, but who's to say I couldn't indulge? Nothing. Nothing is stopping me, other than the fact he might be a serial killer. As long as his chosen weapon is the hard cock pressing into my stomach, I don't think I'd mind so much.

I jerk back and he lets go, though there's a reluctance in his eyes. "Why the knife?"

"Just protecting what's mine. We don't have to use it." His face breaks into a grin and his fingers stroke my jaw before gripping my chin lightly. "Unless you'd like to experiment. You'll find there are very few things I would deny you."

Chapter Six

Xavier

I wish I could erase the indecision in her eyes. There's only so much I can say to convince her. And it isn't the right time to tell her about the curse. She'd run, and while the need to chase her still sits in my chest, I need her to be willing. I won't be like Chad, threatening and taking without regard. She deserves more than that.

Her head tilts, dark hair framing her face. "What *would* you deny me?"

I narrow my eyes, wondering where she's going with this line of questioning. "Nothing specific comes to mind, although I don't particularly care for food in the bedroom."

Her lips part, tongue darting out, and my cock hardens, though I'm not sure how much more I can take in that regard. Being close to her overwhelms my common sense. She has no idea how she affects me. It's as if I manifested her exactly when I needed her. I would have spent the night searching for a way out of here. I wonder if the same force that cursed me drew her back to the theatre.

"That's your limit? No chocolate sauce on your balls?" she exclaims, and I choke. "There has to be something else. What about wax? Or...or peeing?"

"We seem to have gotten a bit off topic, Melody. I'm sure my proclivities run much wilder than yours. You tell me your limits, and I shall acquiesce." I bow my head, and she gives me a look I can't decipher. "Is there something amiss?"

"People don't speak like that anymore. Are you doing a bit?"

"Perhaps you'd like to walk. It seems you have questions before you'll allow me to seduce your body into the pleasure it so desperately craves."

I hold out my hand. A calm spreads through me as her indecision dissolves and she laces her fingers with mine. I tug her, and her mouth forms a perfect O as she stumbles into me. I catch her around the waist, dragging her body alongside mine.

"Better close your mouth before I change my mind about being a gentleman."

She swallows, her throat bobbing with the force, and my fingers tingle, itching to wrap around the elegant column. When her lip finds its way between her teeth, I'm certain she's doing everything on purpose to drive me mad. Perhaps my Melody isn't so innocent after all. I'll gladly allow her to play whatever part she chooses, whether it be seductress or naive waif.

"Let's get you into something more comfortable, hmm?"

Concern flashes in her eyes as I lead her into the greenroom. Searching through the various costumes left behind, I finally find the perfect dress. I present it to her and her mouth drops open. She snaps it shut when she finds my gaze fixated on her lips. She snatches the dress from me, holding the fabric in front of her as she eyes me.

"Are you going to leave while I change?" she snaps, raising her eyebrow.

"Let me know when you need help with the stays." I brush my fingers over her jaw as I make my way out the door.

Several minutes pass while she mutters expletives behind the wood. The dress I chose reminds me of my own time. It will take all my self-control to behave, I'm quite certain. With another curse, she calls to me, and I sweep into the room.

Her hair flies around her head as she spins, glaring at me. Licking my lips, I attempt to keep my racing heart in check. It doesn't work. All she needs to do is drop the hand at her chest and she'll be left gloriously naked. She must sense the lust radiating from me since she huffs.

"This contraption is not worth it. It has more layers than a Napoleon cake, and I have no idea if my legs are in the right place."

"It will decidedly be worth it. And while I haven't eaten a Napoleon cake in some time, I believe this dress does not contain pastry of any sort." I twirl my finger and she spins around, presenting me with her bare back.

I grip my cock, adjusting myself before stepping closer. Her breath hitches as I run my knuckles along her spine, then tie the stays of the dress. I can't keep my hands off her. Being close to her is still overwhelming, yet I can't stop touching her.

When I cinch the last one, she stumbles into me. I press my hand to her stomach to steady her, and she shudders again. I don't have shoes for her, though I doubt she'd put them on. This will have to do. I spin her, running my gaze down her body. She's practically spilling from the neckline, and I lick my lips.

I could have her melting under my touch within minutes. Instead, I pull her from the room and along the corridor toward the orchestra pit. I thought of taking her to my space in the attic, but I fear she's not ready for that. The secret passageways are out of the question. I won't reveal those until she confesses that her body belongs to me for however long I want. The box—my box—though, will be perfect. She'll experience the theatre in a whole new way. Especially if she gives in to me.

"Where are we going?" she gasps as I duck behind the curtain.

"Just a little detour," I murmur as I find the panel I want, then flip the correct switches and spin a dial. Thankfully, they haven't upgraded the mechanics of my theatre when it comes to the tunnels. I'm convinced they don't even know they exist.

When we reach the hidden stairwell to my box, I step back,

presenting the way. She hesitates, then picks up her dress and proceeds upward. She reaches the top and gasps, hand flying to her parted mouth. Slowly, she approaches the railing just as the lights blaze to life over the stage. The set from the last production fills the space, and strains of music echo through the theatre.

Pressing my chest to her back as she wraps her fingers around the railing, I inhale deeply, pulling her sweet scent into my lungs. I cage her in, placing my hands on either side of hers.

I run my nose along the column of her neck. "Enchanting."

"It is. I didn't even know this box existed," she murmurs.

I let out a soft chuckle. "I wasn't speaking of the theatre. And this is my private box. No one is allowed here without my express permission."

She whimpers as I nip at her earlobe, then pull it into my mouth. "I shouldn't."

"Why not? What's holding you back?"

"You're a stranger. I don't understand what's happening, which means this might be a dream. Or maybe I'm drugged, and this is just a hallucination. I don't think my imagination is this vivid, but who knows?" Her head tips back, resting on my shoulder.

"If it's a dream, then why not live out your fantasies? I can assure you, though, I am much more than a figment of your imagination."

I continue my quest to map every inch of her skin with my mouth. She doesn't resist, merely gripping the metal beneath her fingers tighter with each pass of my lips. The idea of christening my box with this exquisite creature is almost my undoing.

"Promise you won't hurt me," she whispers, her head rolling toward me.

Rage that she ever has to worry about something like that boils within my gut. "I vow to never hurt you. Anyone who dares will forfeit their life at my hands."

Her eyes find mine, searching my face for a lie. She won't find one. I'd sooner cut off my own hand before harming her. Even the idea of such a thing fills me with a wrath I've never felt before. Melody would never have to worry again if she allowed me to protect her. Her lip slips between her teeth once more, pulling my gaze down. She releases the plump flesh and sways into me.

Fear flashes in her brilliant blue eyes. "What about Chad?"

"Let him try to come for you. I'll rip his limbs from his body. I'll remove his least valuable asset to society and shove it down his throat. He'll choke on his own dick while I force him to watch as I make your body sing. Unless, of course, you'd like to kill him yourself. In that case, I'll assist you however you require." Bloodlust streaks through my veins, igniting a fury deep within me.

"That's the nicest thing someone has ever said to me." She faces forward, dropping her chin. "Why the hell is that sweet?"

I slide my hand up her arm, to her shoulder, then to her throat, forcing her head back again. "Because it's a testament to how far I would go for you. Only for you, my sweet Melody."

When I squeeze gently, she moans. She rubs her ass along my cock, and spots dance in my vision. It's been so long since I've been this close to another living, breathing human. To have it be Melody—I wonder if this is a fantasy *I've* dreamt up. Maybe I'm merely subsisting within my own hallucination. If it is, I hope I never wake up. Existing for an eternity with her in my arms would be as close to ecstasy as I'll ever come.

"Fuck it," she whispers, and I blink the shadows from my eyes.

"You'll have to be more clear. What exactly does 'fuck it' mean?" I've heard fuck me. And, of course, fuck you. I've never encountered her unique pairing.

She giggles, spinning in my arms, and my hand falls away from her throat to grip the railing. My nostrils flare as I realize how far the bar comes up her back. The height is perfect to bend her over, fingers gripping the metal as I pound into her. Her musical laugh echoes through the air again, and I close my eyes, relishing the sound. It fills what little of my soul is left with a warmth I've never experienced.

"It means why not? Or I don't care about the consequences

anymore." She leans back and I slide my leg between hers, steadying her with my arm.

"There are very few consequences to allowing me to seduce you. Unless you count never experiencing the heights to which I can bring you ever again." I duck my head to nuzzle her neck.

Her skin glides under my teeth, and I ache to mark her as mine. No one would dare touch her, here or in the outside world, if she carried the physical evidence of our coupling. It would be a constant reminder to her as well. Frustration twists through me at the fact we only have tonight. I shove it away, concentrating on the soft noises coming from her.

"Seduce away, mystery man," she breathes.

"Xavier. Tattoo it on your heart. Remember it for when you scream out your release. There's no one to hear you but me, and I crave your pleasure."

She gasps and I cover her mouth with mine, sweeping my tongue along hers. Gripping the back of her neck, I tilt her head to deepen the kiss. It's just as I'd imagined. Our connection is more than this, but it's enough for now. The scene that bursts to life behind my lids as I devour her is one I'll cherish for years to come.

This kiss is the warm sun soaking in my skin on a cloudless summer day. It's the balm to my jagged soul long since blackened. It's the song my heart has been yearning for each night. Nothing can compare with this.

She pulls back, panting as she stares at me wide-eyed. "What the fuck was that?"

I grin before kissing her again. Her squeal turns into a moan as I massage her neck. Her gasps fill my ears as I skim my lips down her throat to trace her collarbone. Such an innocent strip of skin, yet so intoxicating. I sink my teeth into the curve of her breast, savoring her whimpers. Her fingers scramble at the ties restraining her.

"Gorgeous," I murmur as she spills from the dress into my waiting palms.

I pull her nipple into my mouth, rolling my tongue over the tight bud. Her fingers dive into my hair and hold me in place. Bold of her to assume I'll be doing anything else for the foreseeable future. The longer I spend worshiping her, the more likely she is to give all of herself over to me. I move to the other, giving it the same attention.

"Turn around," I whisper, my cock twitching as she obeys immediately. "Can you hear it?"

She shakes her head, soft curls of dark hair sliding across her shoulders with the movement. "I don't hear anything."

Gathering the hem of her dress, I grip the many layers and lift them gently. She shudders, her body curving over the railing as she seizes hold of the metal. My palm grazes her bare skin, and I realize she's not wearing anything underneath.

"My naughty little vixen." I stroke her inner thigh, which trembles under my touch. "Tell me, did you take off your panties when you put this dress on, or were you bare the entire time you played this evening?"

"I-I took them o-off," she sputters. "They were d-damp."

I skate my finger to her cunt and slip one between her folds. "You're soaked now, little muse. Is this all for me?"

"Yes," she hisses, wiggling as I skim her flesh. "Please."

I dip my fingertip inside her and she whines. Stroking her slowly, I build her up gradually. I want her on her knees, pleading for my cock in her mouth. I want her ravenous for me to fill her. I want her begging me to make her come. I want her desperate for the relief only I can give.

I place my other hand on the back of her neck and guide her down until her forehead rests on her hands still clutching the bar. Her ass on full display with my fingers deep inside her wet cunt is almost my undoing, and I bite my cheek to keep from pulling out my cock and slamming into her. Her hips sway, meeting me with each thrust. Needy sounds fall from her lips.

Leaning over her, my mouth brushes the shell of her ear. "Do you hear it now, Melody? Your pleasure resonating through the theatre? Give me more. Give voice to your desire and make it rico-chet off the walls."

"Oh God," she wheezes as I pound my fingers into her harder, faster.

A growl leaves me without thought. "Not God, though you're welcome to worship at my feet."

Chapter Seven

Melody

I can't believe I'm doing this. Somehow, I went from hiding from a timpani player turned stalker to being in a private box I never knew existed. Throw in the old-fashioned dress and his fingers buried in my pussy and I'm pretty sure I really am living in a dream. Here's hoping it doesn't turn into a nightmare before he makes me come.

"Oh fuck, please," I moan as he thrusts his fingers into me.

With heaving breaths, I close my eyes, focusing on the pleasure coursing through me. I never thought I'd beg someone, but the words are ripped from me without warning. I can't seem to stop moaning out my pleas. Under normal circumstances, I'd be embarrassed. Instead, I shut my brain off and give myself over to the feelings he conjures.

Xavier's arm loops around my waist, and his fingers find my clit. A shock of electricity hits me, peals of bells ringing in my ears. Tucking my chin to my chest, my orgasm ripples through me. I thought it would be thunderous. I thought it would burn through my veins with its intensity. This is only a hook-up after all. Usually, one-night stands are a flash in the pan and most of the time I don't come. This is something more. Like the rising sun in the morning, casting a soft glow over the world as another day begins anew.

My body droops, a weightlessness overcoming me. Xavier's arm holds me upright as his fingers continue their quest to ring every ounce of pleasure from me. He whispers words of encouragement into my skin, making the hair on the back of my neck stand up. I cry out when he stands upright. He shushes me as if he didn't command me to scream out my release not five minutes ago.

A sound of protest falls unbidden from me when he pulls his hands away. I glance over my shoulder, intending to rip him a new one for leaving me hanging. I want more—a lot more. He raises a single eyebrow, then pops his fingers in his mouth, cheeks hollowing as he cleans them. His eyes fall shut and he groans as if he's savoring the taste.

I never thought of myself as vanilla in bed, but this man is on a whole new level. I've never been with someone who actually enjoys this type of thing. Usually it's wham, bam, thank you ma'am, and I go home to take care of myself with a toy. The ravenous look in Xavier's dark eyes sends a shiver up my spine. I don't know if I'm ready for whatever he has planned for me— for us.

He spins his finger, and I turn back around. My gaze bounces around the theatre and settles on my xylophone. Most of the time, I'm elated to see the instrument. There's a vibration that bounces through me each and every time. I must be too far away to feel it now, though. Instead, I'm hyper aware of Xavier ambling behind me. I can't tell where he is exactly, but I can sense him.

Fabric rustles and my breath stutters as heat builds in my stomach. His gentle touch lights the flame within me again. Holding my breath, I silently beg him to dive between my legs again. He doesn't, much to my dismay.

He grabs the dress, shoving it further up my back. There are so many layers, I'm afraid he'll get lost in them and I'll never get relief.

He presses his body to mine, his hard cock nestling between my legs. "Did you think I'd leave you empty and wanting?"

"Yes," I snap. "Are you going to prove me wrong?"

He chuckles as his hand wraps around my throat and tugs me up until my back is plastered to his chest. He squeezes, forcing my head back. It's not enough to cut off my air and, for some reason I can't fathom, a gush of wetness gathers between my legs. Shit, I actually like this. Clearly, I need to do more exploring with this type of thing. Thankfully, Xavier seems to know exactly what I need.

"Pull up your dress," he growls. The hem already sits at on my hips, allowing me to gather the front and expose my legs. "Higher."

His voice rumbles in his chest, vibrating through me, and I scramble to obey. He hums as his other hand slides to my pussy. I whimper as he plays with me, his fingers flexing around my throat.

"What a wanton creature you are. I knew you would be." His words swirl around me, barely registering as he circles my clit.

"I need..." I can't even finish the sentence I'm so focused on the desire building within me once more.

"Do you need my cock? Do you need me pounding into you, filling you completely over and over and over?" He plunges his fingers into me, punctuating each word with another thrust.

I swallow hard, unsure how to respond. Maybe I can still get what I want without answering. I most certainly do want him pounding into me, but it seems irrational to beg a figment of my imagination to rail me.

Admitting to myself I'm letting a stranger fuck me in an empty theatre will send me over the edge. So I've convinced my mind this is a dream. There's still that small part of me that worries I really have lost the plot and when I come to my senses, I'll be...shameless.

"Use your words, Melody. Tell me what's going on in that pretty little head of yours."

"I want you, but I shouldn't," I mumble.

He sighs and his fingers move from my throat to my jaw, then he nuzzles my neck. His hand stalls between my legs, leaving me bereft.

"Says who? I'll silence whomever tells you we don't deserve this." He doesn't wait for me to respond. "Now, tell me you want my cock."

A beat of silence later and my resolve caves. "I want your cock."

He guides me down once more, pulling his hand away from me to slide to my waist. My dress, still gathered in my fists, cushions my stomach as I lean against the rail. My body is practically hanging over the bar and my heart leaps into my throat.

"Remember my name," he rumbles, his cock nudging my entrance, and I quiver. "You'll be screaming it soon."

He slams into me, stretching me, and I yelp. His ragged breath ghosts along my skin as he covers my body with his. His limbs shake...no, his entire body trembles, and I wonder why he's holding back.

"Move," I moan, pushing back.

"A minute, if you will." He rolls his hips as his fingers dig into my skin.

He's probably leaving bruises behind. If this is truly happening, at least I'll have the physical reminder in the morning. I'll probably mourn the loss when they eventually fade. It's been too long since I've connected with someone else. Perhaps I'll never feel this again.

I clench around him as he rolls his hips again. I'll have to force his hand if he doesn't get his shit together soon. As soon as the thought enters my mind, I freeze.

Music. An undertone of notes snakes through the air and wraps around me. As the first chord rings out, Xavier pulls out almost completely, then slams back into me. He does it again as the harmony builds. When the melody enters, he picks up the pace, burying his cock into me.

"Do you hear it?" he asks through gritted teeth.

I nod, closing my eyes as the composition swells along with the pleasure within me. I give myself over to the sensations, whimpering as he hits just the right spot deep in my pussy.

"Don't stop," I gasp.

"Never, my sweet. Do not come until the crescendo."

He plunges into me harder, and I bite my lip, hoping to hold back the wave of ecstasy threatening to pull me under. No way in hell am I going to hold off just because he wants me to wait for some mystical moment.

"Almost there," he growls as the music layers one measure on top of another.

"I can't..." I whine, and my legs begin to shake.

"You will or there will be consequences."

I throw my head back, too far gone to question him. Finally, what I assume is the crescendo hits and I ride the edge of euphoria, waiting for the beat to drop. Xavier shudders, moaning my name as he crashes into oblivion a minute later.

I clamp my lips together, holding back my cries of pleasure. I drift along, praying he doesn't stop, then shake my head. The music disappears from one note to the next. It's as if everything just shuts off, leaving me struggling through a void.

A heaviness overtakes my body, and my knees give out. It's not the pulsing waves of pleasure. My orgasm hangs just out of reach, refusing to come any closer. Xavier's arm wraps around my waist, holding me upright as I spasm around him once. Not enough.

He grunts, pressing his forehead between my shoulder blades. With a low growl, he pulls from me, leaving an emptiness behind. The experience was like a beautiful song, notes woven together to create magic. But the last discordant note was wrong, causing a sourness to invade my senses.

"You've got to be fucking kidding me," I breathe even as I have the irrational urge to cry.

Tears fill my eyes and I straighten, pushing my dress down. The ties in the front almost prevent me from shoving my tits back in and my nipple catches on the neckline. I swallow down the yelp of pain. This night has decided to go to hell in a handbasket, and I'm done with it all.

Whatever the hell just happened between us doesn't matter. We're not having an encore. This isn't what I signed up for. Actually, I didn't even put my name on the list. I got caught up in the grandeur and mystery of tonight. Anything to take my mind off the nightmare Chad created.

And now it's done. I'll merely walk out of here and go stay at a hotel. Not that I have that kind of money. The threat of Chad waiting for me is too dire to run home, but that doesn't mean I have to stay here.

I wipe the wetness from my face, grimacing as the evidence of my decisions stains my thighs. I won't be able to erase my memories so easily. Part of me won't let it go, and I fear it'll be a long time before that music filters to the back of my mind. I'll hear it as I fall asleep, the haunting melody flitting through the air. I'll constantly be searching for how it should end, though.

Xavier growls behind me, and I steal a glance over my shoulder. Dark fabric stretches over his back as he runs his fingers through his hair, frustration incarnate. His muscles bunch as he grips the strands, and I peek at the door.

Sliding toward the exit, I keep my eyes on him. I'm not scared of Xavier, no matter the questions I had before. For some reason, I know he'd let me go if I wanted to leave. I have absolutely no evidence to support that, but I'm going with my gut. He wouldn't hurt me, but I'd rather not have the conversation about how our encounter started out hot and ended in a lackluster fashion.

My hand wraps around the handle, and I freeze as he clears his throat.

"Going somewhere, Melody?"

I exhale sharply through my nose, pressing my lips together. Being caught sneaking out will make this even more awkward. I don't bother turning around, instead addressing the door.

"It's getting late." I doubt he'll let me get away with such a flimsy excuse.

"Ah," he exclaims softly. "Perhaps you didn't hear me before."

The edge in his voice has me whipping around and crossing my arms over my chest. "Which part exactly are you referring to? The part where you said you'd take me to heights I've never seen before? Or the one where you commanded me not to come until some arbitrary point in time only you were aware of?"

He raises an eyebrow as he adjusts his cuffs. He studies my face before his gaze sweeps down my body, then up again. I can't read him no matter how hard I try. I start counting when he doesn't speak, telling myself I'll give him a full minute. If he doesn't start talking, I'll merely leave. At sixty seconds, I sigh.

"For one night, you belong to me. And I have something for you."

I roll my eyes. "And what's that?"

He smirks, stepping closer. "Your punishment."

Chapter Eight

Xavier

I love the look of shock as it flits across her face. I'm sure she thought I would just allow her to walk out without a word. She'll learn eventually that I mean what I say. She'll learn to follow the timing I set, a maestro conducting her pleasure until our composition is complete.

She snorts, glancing away. "You think after that I'm going to let you punish me? And I never said I belong to you."

"Your cunt did when she clung to my cock. And a punishment, by definition, is not something one lets happen. It merely is." I saunter closer to her, and her fingers tighten on the handle. "Surely you're not satisfied walking away so early in the night?"

Her throat bobs and my cock hardens. The curse doesn't allow me gratification for long. As long as I can convince Melody to stay, I'll be able to fuck her all night long.

"This was a fun little experiment, but—"

"Did you hear the symphony?" I ask, and she jolts. "Our symphony, my little muse."

Her lips part, eyes taking on a faraway look. "Why do you call me that?"

"I'll show you," I whisper, holding out my hand to her. I'll wait as long as it takes for her to decide. Decades have passed as

I've anticipated her arrival. A few more minutes won't make a difference.

"Are you going to leave me without an orgasm again?"

I smile, though her words are anything but funny. She scowls and I take one more step. She pulls in a deep breath, her beautiful tits brushing my chest. Running a finger down her jaw, I watch the flush travel up her neck to her cheeks.

"There's an explanation if you're capable of staying put."

Her body sways toward me, and I lace our fingers together. She doesn't seem to notice.

"Why the hell are you grinning?" she huffs.

I lean into her, pressing a light kiss to her cheek. "You're much more spirited than I expected. I find I enjoy it. Let me show you my world."

I hold my breath as she searches my eyes. Something deep within me settles into place, suspiciously close to my heart. If my words alone would convince her, I'd use them. If a simple touch from me would sway her to my side, I'd spend hours caressing her. If staring into her eyes could persuade her, I would stay right here as long as need be.

"Fine, maestro. Show me."

"Be careful. Calling me such things could very well go to my head."

I reach around her and place my hand on hers to open the door. Her body trembles, not as unaffected as she'd have me believe. Her bravado is lovely, though unnecessary.

It takes me a minute to gather the courage to slip through the hidden panel across the staircase from my private box. Showing her not one, but two secrets, may be too much for her. It can't be helped. I'll bring her to my attic—my safe haven.

I spend the time we ascend discarding each punishment I dream up. She's clearly not ready for most of them, though maybe by the end of the night she'll allow me.

Stopping outside the thick wooden door, my heart skips a beat. I've known since the first time Melody played my xylophone that she was mine. Showing her my inner sanctum, the only place I've felt truly comfortable even before I was cursed, sends a terrifying thrill through me. I shove all the doubts and questions of whether she'll like it aside.

Pushing it open, I step back and sweep out my hand to usher her inside. My chest seizes as she steps over the threshold, then pauses. I close my eyes, unable to watch her gaze bounce around the room.

Swallowing hard, I shake my head, silently scolding myself for being like this. My eyes fly open, and I stride forward to press my chest against her back. She sucks in a sharp breath but doesn't move away.

I wrap my arm around her waist and hold her close. Dipping down, I graze my lips behind her ear. She shivers and tilts her head, exposing more of her delicious skin to my ministrations.

For all her words before, she's giving in quite easily. Soon enough she'll understand what happened in the box and why her body craves me even while her mind rebels. She'll understand why she didn't reach a rapturous ending.

"What do you think?" I murmur into her flesh.

"I never knew this was up here. Why all the masks?" She leans into me, muscles relaxing as I latch onto her earlobe and nibble.

"I've been collecting them for...a while." I clear my throat as I straighten. I'm unable to release her so soon, but her questions won't be easy to answer without revealing more than she's ready for.

"Do you wear them? They have strings. Can I put one on?" She stiffens and attempts to put distance between us. "Sorry, that was..."

I chuckle as I step next to her and grab her hand. Tugging her toward the masks, I scan them, looking for one in particular. I pluck a masquerade one from the wall, my fingers slipping through the black feathers jutting from one corner. She twitches as I slide it over her face. The delicate lace frames her eyes, accentuating her cheekbones.

"Exquisite," I breathe. I grip her chin with my fingers and skim my lips over hers.

"This doesn't answer any of my questions." Annoyance weaves its way through her voice, and I pull back.

I spin her around and point as I rest my cheek against her hair. A grand piano that took me ages to get up here through a series of gears and pulleys sits in the corner of the room. I haven't had the time nor the inclination to clean up the space, and sheets of music litter the area.

Slowly, she weaves her way around the furniture toward the instrument. One by one, she scans the various half-filled pieces of paper. A quill and inkwell sit precariously on the rack next to my masterpiece, and her finger brushes the feather.

"Is this...are you writing a symphony?" She peers at me, a curious expression gracing her face.

"Our symphony."

As I approach, she turns to me. She stiffens, then shuffles toward the door. She's trying to be surreptitious about it, but I know her better. I've said too much. Or not enough. Either way, I am now the man she fears. Perhaps I should have explained about our connection, though I am certain she will keep running if I tell her the truth about me.

I freeze, tucking my hands behind my back. "Perhaps you'd like an explanation?"

"An explanation of how you lured me here, fucked me, then somehow have been watching me closely enough to write a whole fucking concerto based on some mysterious connection we have? No, thank you." Even with the diatribe she's spewing, she's stopped attempting to sidle to the exit.

"Yes, well. As you recall, I did not *lure* you here. You came of your own volition, several times, I might add." I smirk, but she doesn't return the sentiment.

"I only came once."

"Perhaps next time you should follow directions." I clear my throat as I sober. "That being said, the truth will undoubtedly be more complicated to grasp."

"Is that a fancy way of saying you think I'm stupid?" Her fists land on her hips and she cocks her head.

"Absolutely not. However, I feel as if this is a little out of the realm of understanding for most people who are not a bit superstitious."

My heart pounds in my chest, wondering if I can really go through with this. I'll lose her for sure if I do. She deserves to know, no matter how I crave to be deep in her cunt again. No matter how my soul will long for hers as the lonely years pass. If all we have is the few hours we've already filled, then so be it.

"Well, go ahead then."

My lips twitch as I regard her. With her scolding me in a dress the likes of which this world hasn't seen in centuries and a beautiful mask gracing her face, it's almost too much to take in. She scowls and I clear my throat. This would be easier with a glass of bourbon in hand. I doubt she'd allow me such a luxury.

I open my mouth, intending to get straight to the point when a gong sounds out. My head whips to the side, and I'm moving before I've made the conscious decision to do so. She squeaks as I pass, and I pivot to grip her upper arms.

"Stay here. Do not leave this room." I squeeze to emphasize how important it is for her to listen.

"What the hell was that?"

"An early alarm system. I had it installed when the theatre was built. It's the only thing that works if someone uses modern ways to enter," I say quickly. Her eyes widen the more I tell her. "I do not have the time to explain everything. But you must stay here in order for me to deal with him."

"Him?" she squeaks. "Chad?"

I nod sharply. "Your word, Melody. Stay here."

She nods absentmindedly, her gaze wandering over my shoulder toward the door. I let out a curse under my breath, then grab her hand and tug her after me.

"I thought you wanted me to stay there?" she whispers, fear lacing her tone.

"I doubt you will listen, so you must come with me. It's the only way to keep you safe." We rush through the hidden stairwells, her cursing every few steps. Perhaps the dress wasn't such a good idea. I didn't think Chad would follow her back here, though. No matter how much I wished he would. I assumed he'd give up when she didn't go home. Then again, I didn't assume she'd be here either.

"Why the hell wouldn't I obey something like that?" she hisses as we reach a landing.

I spin, caging her against the wall, and she gasps. "Maybe because you didn't the last time I gave you a command?"

Her mouth drops open and annoyance bubbles out of her. "You can't honestly believe a stalker coming after me and you telling me not to orgasm are on the same level of importance."

"Oh, my sweet." I wrap my fingers around her throat and desire washes her irritation away. "Your pleasure is of greatest importance to me. This prick is merely a small inconvenience I'll rectify shortly. Then we can get back to stoking the flames still burning within you."

"We're not done with this conversation," she spits out as I release her.

"Of course not. Merely delayed, my sweet little Melody." I grab her hand again and tug her through a doorway.

"Shit, shit, shit. That wasn't there before," she mutters. She clutches at me, practically climbing my back.

I rush her through the dark, hyperaware of each dip and turn. She stumbles after me even with my guidance. I'm tempted to throw her over my shoulder for the rest of the journey, but I fear that would slow us down more.

"Where are we going?" she hisses as we take one last turn.

"The alarm was for the back door. He won't be able to get through, as you found out earlier. I assume he'll opt for the front. Unless you have a better idea of where he'd go?"

"The orchestra entrance. It's on the east side of the building. On the other side of the greenroom."

I change directions, and she yelps as I yank her with me. I'd rather stalk him through the halls, torturing him with fear much like he's wrought upon Melody. With her following me, though, I won't subject her to such violence. I'll spare her from encountering the vicious beast lurking beneath my skin. To hell with my curse—she'd run screaming from me if she watched me systematically take Chad apart bit by bit.

"You have your knife, right?" she wheezes as we stutter to a stop in front of one last door.

"Yes, why?" I glance over my shoulder, and she smirks.

"You promised to protect me from him. I assumed that meant you'd kill him if need be."

We don't have time for a tête-à-tête. However, the glint in her eye intrigues me enough to face her.

"And would you like me to make him pay?" I brush my thumb over her lip, plucking at the flesh.

"If I thought I could, I'd tear him apart with my bare hands. Though I suspect you'll have more fun doing that than I would."

I grin, gripping her neck and pulling her close. "My, my. What a delectably villainous creature you are."

Chapter Nine

Melody

Electricity courses through my body, lighting me up from the inside out. A twinge of doubt filters through the exhilaration, and my foot trips over a cord as I pull away from him. Xavier is there before I have time to blink, catching me around the waist.

"Sorry," I mumble as he rights me.

"What's that look?" he growls, whipping his head around. We *are* standing in the middle of the hallway by the greenroom. Chad could be anywhere.

"Are we sure he's a stalker? What if he's just—"

"Don't tell me you're getting cold feet, Melody." His dark eyes bore into mine. "He followed you. He threatened you."

My heart pounds in my chest. "Why do you care so much?"

His nostrils flare and a vein in his forehead pops out. "He touched what was mine. And now he pays for his sins at the end of my knife."

He releases me to stalk down the hallway in search of Chad. I hurry after him as my stomach flips. I never thought I'd be into the whole possessive thing, especially when we're stalking a stalker. Clearly, we have other things to do, but my insides are tingling, and my thighs are a little more than damp.

"What the fuck is wrong with me?" I say under my breath.

Xavier sends me a smirk over his shoulder. "Did that make you wet, little muse? Don't worry. There's nothing wrong with you. I'll take care of you after we've dealt with this little problem."

Trying to rub my legs together while I'm running after him in a froofy dress is probably the hardest thing I've ever done. I don't know where we're going or how Xavier can tell where Chad is. I'm just along for the ride. Maybe I should have stayed in the attic. It was creepy yet had a lived-in feel to it. I still can't figure out who or what he is. There are probably some clues in his room.

Xavier throws out his arm, stopping me just before we round the corner to another hallway. He peers into the dark and huffs. I attempt to peek around him, but he holds me back. Rolling my eyes, I lean against the wall and wait. It only gives me more time to start wondering if I've made the wrong decision.

"Are we just going to wait until he stumbles upon us?" I mumble, imitating his slight accent. It's old-fashioned and hard to place, but apparently I don't do it justice since he grunts.

"Wandering around the theatre will only put us at a disadvantage."

"I thought he was a 'little problem.' Change your mind?"

He scowls, seizing my hand, and tugs me back toward the orchestra pit. We crouch behind the stage and scan the area. There's no sign of Chad. I wonder if he was even here to begin with. The alarm system seems archaic.

I tug away from him, setting my feet before he can pull me up the small staircase where my instrument is set up. He glances back at me, annoyance on his face.

"Is this some ploy?" I ask, my doubts swamping me.

He swings around, then gestures me closer to the back wall. It's not very sturdy construction since it's merely to separate the curtains from the back area. If I have to run, I'll probably be able to crash right through it. I'm hesitant to lean on it like I want, though. The corset of the dress digs into my ribs, making it hard to breathe. I rip the mask from my face, dropping it at my feet. He scowls at the lace as if he's personally offended I've removed the thing.

"Why exactly would I fabricate—"

The emergency lights cut out and I gasp, latching onto Xavier. He grips my arms and pushes me back to the wall with a mumbled curse. The air conditioner cuts out and silence blankets us. Only our harsh breathing echoes through the empty space. His lips brush the shell of my ear, sending a shiver through me.

"Stay here," he whispers, and I shake my head, though he can't see me. "I'll be mere feet away. Do not be afraid."

Slowly, I unclench my fingers one by one until he slips from my grasp. My emotions bounce from frustration to fear within the span of seconds. I expect him to come back right away, but he doesn't. Before long, my mind starts playing tricks on me.

I press my back against the partition as I glance around, trying to pierce the darkness. I never thought of the theatre as creepy, yet here we are. First the mysterious private box, then the hidden tunnels, and an attic no one has seen in decades. Throw in a dark, eerie orchestra pit and I'm tapped out. Nothing could have prepared me for the shit that's happened tonight. I feel like I'm in an alternate dimension.

I gasp when a thought hits me. Maybe I am dreaming. Or hallucinating. Maybe I went home, and Chad was waiting for me and kidnapped me and drugged me, and I have no idea what's real. I brace my hands on my knees, the corset preventing me from pulling in a full breath.

Maybe I'm dead.

Maybe I'm dead and my memories are weaving with some strange fantasy, refusing to let me cross over. Am I cursed? Will I go back to Xavier's attic and fall asleep in that ridiculous large bed complete with a canopy framing the whole thing, only to wake up to yet another rendition of my last night on earth? I don't know how many times I can live this scenario and I haven't even gotten through the first go around.

Someone's arm slips around my shoulders, and I yelp. A hand

covers my mouth, cutting off the next scream. A man's body leans into mine, hot breath ghosting across my forehead.

"Shh, it's me," Xavier hisses, and a sob escapes me.

Tears fill my eyes as I straighten. When I blink, they streak down my face, gathering on his skin, and he curses softly.

"It's okay. I'm here. I won't leave you again," he murmurs, wrapping his arms around me.

Even if he is a mirage, my mind has conjured from some deep recess of my psyche, I still cling to him. I bury my face into his chest, trying to cut off my breakdown before it becomes a full-on panic attack. Neither of us needs that. His hand threads through my hair as he shushes me. His low voice is soothing in a way I don't understand.

Once I have my shit together, I'll let go. But this blasted dress isn't making it any easier. As if he's read my mind, he undoes the knot resting on my lower back, then plucks at the ties. They loosen bit by bit until I can suck in a full breath.

His thumbs brush away the wetness on my cheeks. "Better?"

"Yes. Sorry. Did you find him?"

"I believe so. He was calling for you in the back. He'll make his way here eventually. Tell me, Melody, have you calmed yourself enough to lure him here?"

A ticking noise fills the air, and my body stiffens, though whether from his question or the sudden sound, I don't know. Could I be bait? Probably. I'm equal parts terrified and pissed off when it comes to Chad. I tried to be nice and reject him. He wouldn't take no for an answer. That's on him. Coaxing him into the open, to his death, shouldn't be a problem. As long as Xavier actually does what he says he will.

A second later, the lights under the stage flare to life. They're old and barely pierce the darkness surrounding us, but it's enough to make out Xavier's expression. Concern lines his eyes and he cups my face. With a gentleness I didn't think he possessed, he kisses me. A delicate melody flutters through the air and peace steals through me.

He pulls back, resting his forehead against mine. "Do not concern yourself with it. I shall take care of him."

My lip slips between my teeth. "Why do you sound like you're from a different time? People don't talk like that anymore."

He flashes me a grin. "Perhaps I *am* from another time. Now, hide beneath the risers."

He leads me forward, but I balk. "I don't want to hide. I'll be the bait. Do you have a gun?"

Glancing around, he runs his fingers through his dark hair. "They are cumbersome things. I prefer to exact justice with a personal flair."

"Have you done this a lot? How many others have you done this for?"

Maybe this is a game for him. I'm still ping-ponging between trusting him and positive he's about to kill me. Yet not quite. If I truly felt in danger, I never would have stayed here. I certainly wouldn't have allowed him to fuck me. And I wouldn't be wearing this ridiculous dress.

He tracks the emotions flitting across my face, a small smile settling on his lips by the time I've concluded I'm in no danger from this man.

"Would you still like me to answer?" His thumb plucks at my bottom lip.

"Just tell me you're qualified to do this." It's a demand, and from the look in his eyes, he knows it.

"Anything for you, my sweet."

In the span of a blink, he's gone, prowling up the stairs to the stage. He turns, gesturing me to follow, and I chase after him. He stops in the middle of the space and points at the tape on the floor marking a long-forgotten cue. Dutifully, I stand gazing through the muted light at the rows of seats. Scanning the balcony, I find nothing. Unless Chad has ducked behind a single chair or laid his body out on a row of them, he's not here.

When my gaze returns to the stage, Xavier is gone. My heart jumps in my chest and my hands tremble, the urge to vomit creeping up my throat. I spot him in the orchestra pit below me, weaving his way through the chairs and musical stands.

My xylophone sits to my right, a fracture of light reflecting off the bars. The pull I usually feel has disappeared, or rather, transferred to Xavier. I bite my cheek, eyes bouncing between him and the instrument. There's something I'm missing. It dances just out of reach, taunting me with the revelations it holds. Shaking my head, I fix my mind on the crisis at hand.

I have no idea how I'm supposed to lure Chad here. I whip my head around, afraid he's snuck up behind me, but no one is there. This is almost worse than standing in the dark. At least then I knew he wouldn't be able to see me just as much as I couldn't see him. There was comfort in the blackness. With the subdued lighting, I'm on edge, just waiting for a blade to swipe across my throat.

Swallowing hard, I twist my fingers together, pinching the skin of my knuckles. I hoped the small bite of pain would center me, but all it does is make me more nervous. I open my mouth to call out to Xavier when a spotlight blares to life, blinding me. Tucking my chin to my chest, I take a single step back. The old black-painted wood shines under the sudden illumination, giving me the sensation that it's moving, like small waves rippling under my feet.

I dig my nails into my bare arm while I slowly lift my head. I can barely make out the first few rows and I squint my eyes. It doesn't do any good. Someone starts a slow clap, each sound echoing through the space. It's a death keel ringing inside my head. Xavier is nowhere to be seen. A small voice inside me screams *run*. As if I'd make it very far.

Chad steps into the light, making his way down the center aisle. "You led me on a merry little chase, Melody."

"As if I'd put any energy into your game, Chad." My voice shakes, but at least I'm not a blubbering mess.

He smiles sadistically. I never noticed the cruel edge in his eyes, or the malicious tilt of his chin. He masked it well enough.

Or maybe I just didn't want to see it. I spent so long plodding along with my head down, I never saw the signs. I'm tired of being nice to men so they won't hurt me. Now I'm stuck in this situation, and I have no one to blame but myself. And Chad, of course. He's ultimately at fault and I need to remember that.

"Some games are played without the participants being aware. Are you going to be a good girl and stop running?" Chad drops into a chair in the first row and crosses his legs. "Perhaps you'd like to put on a show for me first? You certainly dressed for the part."

I plant my fists on my hips. "I'd rather not. But I'm sure the police will be happy to know all about your pursuit of me and how unwelcome it actually is."

He chuckles as he rubs his jaw, then settles his gaze on me. "I haven't touched you. Haven't hurt you...yet. They'll do as they always do—nothing. And by the time you have something to report, you'll no longer be in a position to contradict me."

"That sounds like a threat." My voice wavers, my fear peeking through my false bravado.

He sits forward, dropping his elbows on his knees. "That's a promise, bunny. Now why don't you hop away so we can finish this the way it was always meant to be."

Chapter Ten

Xavier

I wish I could stab the timpani. It's right here in front of me and would be easy enough. My sharp knife would glide right through the skin stretched across the top. Then I could fill the drum with Chad's blood and drown him in it.

I shake my head, banishing the images from my mind. Melody may have a dark streak inside of her, but she wouldn't appreciate seeing something as gruesome as that. I'm sure it's why she asked if I possessed a gun. It would take too long to reload, should the bullet run afoul. It would be a cleaner kill, though.

As I crouch behind the percussion section in the back of the pit, I track Chad's movements. Every taunt that falls from his mouth sends a bolt of rage through me. I wish I'd had more time to prepare Melody for her role in this. Actually, I wish she would have stayed in my room. Hell, I'd take my box if it meant keeping her away from Chad's prying eyes.

As his gaze rakes her body, I'm also regretting the dress I had her wear. Truly, I didn't believe he'd come here. And if he did, I didn't believe he'd have access to the theatre. I wonder who allowed him such freedoms. He hasn't been around more than half a year, based on all the performances I've lived through while wallowing in the xylophone.

Perhaps there's some other explanation. The impostor owners of the theatre certainly aren't upstanding gentlemen. They've practically let the building fall into disrepair. If it wasn't for me, they would have been shut down long ago. And I'd never hear the music or see Melody again. I can't bear that.

"I don't need to run from you, Chad. You're going to leave and never come back. You're going to stop following women who *clearly* have no interest. In fact, you should move to the middle of the goddamn woods and be celibate for the rest of your life. It's the decent thing to do."

Chad scoffs, just like I knew he would. Such arrogance comes from never being held in check. While Melody's tactics aren't what I would choose, at least she's keeping him occupied. Men like him always like to gloat. If she can rile him up, he'll make a mistake. Then I might be able to stop her from seeing any of the gory details of what I do to him.

"You don't seem to understand the situation you're in, Melody. We're in an empty theatre—hours before anyone is set to come back. I know this place much better than you ever could. There's nowhere for you to hide. You can't outrun me. Can't overpower me. You're trapped in a maze, and it would only be a matter of time before I caught you. Do you really want to tire yourself doing all of that? Then you wouldn't have the energy to fight me." Chad grins, adjusting himself as if the thought of her fighting him excites him.

My lip curls at the thought of him touching her. This has gone on too long. The space between us, even if I snuck to the front of the pit, is too great. Melody's questions about a gun made me wonder if Chad has one. I won't risk him injuring me enough to be unable to protect her. Leaving her vulnerable isn't an option. I promised to take care of this piece of shit, and I intend to do so.

A bullet won't kill me. Hell, he could riddle my body with them and I wouldn't die. I'd tried to end my suffering many times over the years, desperate to escape this prison. The results were intense pain, and the next thing I knew, I was encased in the xylophone once more. Now I wonder if whoever cursed me knew I'd one day meet the one who would light me up—the one meant to save me. Perhaps they anticipated a scenario just like this.

Melody snorts. "Oh, so you know about the basement, then?"

My head whips around, trying to spot her. The stage covers most of her body, especially since she's been creeping backward. I never told her about the basement. Several of the tunnels lead there, but even as we were racing through them, I didn't say anything. She's probably bluffing. It's the only explanation. The cavernous basement has been sealed off for decades now. No one knows of the secret entrances found in the tunnels to reach the lake. I doubt anyone has been down there other than me in centuries.

"Nice try," Chad says, smirking.

Her eyebrows climb higher and she shrugs innocently. "Believe me or not, but it's there. Complete with hidden alcoves and various waterways. From what I remember, there's even a hidden exit. But I'm sure you're not worried about me finding that."

Chad's nostrils flare and he pushes from his chair. "You lie. I won't tolerate lying, Melody."

"As if I care about what you'll tolerate," she snaps. "You can fuck off, Chad. If you keep it up, the only way you'll be leaving is in a body bag."

"Where would you get a body bag? Do you plan on lugging me out of here? All five and a half feet of you?" His head falls back, and he barks out a laugh.

He approaches the railing blocking the seats from the orchestra. I've seen more than one drunken patron tip ass over end into the space in my time. It's the reason they set the director's podium closer to the stage.

Staying crouched, I slide closer to him and slip my knife from the sheath at my waist. Silently, I plead with Melody to keep his attention focused on her.

"You underestimate me, Chad. While normally you'd be correct that I am in no condition to take you on, you forget."

My gaze darts to her, meeting her eyes briefly before hers bounce back to Chad. Her cue is clear, and I hurry forward, ducking behind the bass drums for cover.

"Forget what, bunny? That you like the chase? That you're mine and no one is here to save you?"

I'm feet from him now, hidden behind the grand piano. Chad spreads his arms wide, gesturing to the supposedly empty area around him. He slips a knife from his pocket and drops it. The point sticks in the floor, handle wobbling.

He splays his hands again. "I'm no longer armed. Does that give you more incentive to give in?"

I have no idea why getting rid of a singular blade she didn't know existed is supposed to have her crumbling at his feet. She pales and her hands slide down her dress. The move definitely didn't put her at ease. I glance around again, loath to take my eyes off him. I need a way to get to him without alerting him before the time is right. None of this is going the way I hoped.

I grin when Chad jumps into the pit, then steps onto the director's riser. His hands curl around the music stand, and he leans forward. If he falls, I won't be able to contain my laughter. It might break the fear building in Melody. Unfortunately, he doesn't. He just rocks back and forth as if he's having a delightful conversation with her instead of sharing his nefarious plans.

Melody flicks her chin up and narrows her eyes. "We're alone?"

Chad laughs, throwing his head back. I use the distraction to slip around the piano and come up behind him. The riser creaks as I step onto it gently. He's moving too much to notice it isn't his own feet creating the noise.

I grip my knife tighter and my eyes meet Melody's over his shoulder. Her lip slips between her teeth, and I shake my head. I need her to keep up the charade just a little longer. She releases her flesh, and my cock throbs. She's a walking sinful desire. I doubt one night will be enough with her.

"Of course we're alone," Chad sneers, straightening.

I slip my knife to his throat, my frame towering over his by at least six inches. He stiffens and my muscles coil, waiting for him to lash out.

"Are you sure about that?" I whisper.

His body trembles and my lip curls. Disgusting creature. He preys on those he deems weak, unable to keep his bowels in check when a real threat appears. He'll beg and plead for mercy at some point.

My eyes find Melody's. "What should we do with him, little muse?"

A shiver flows through her as she steps to the edge of the stage. "I want him to confess."

I dig the edge of the blade farther into his skin. Blood trickles from the wound left behind.

"You heard my lady. Confess your sins. Then petition for clemency. Perhaps she'll allow you to atone for your sins, though I doubt you'll be able to absolve yourself to my satisfaction, much less hers."

"Who the hell are you?" Chad spits out when he finds his voice.

"Your executioner. I trust you realize how fucked you truly are. You'd do well to obey her."

He swallows, the blade scraping against his skin. I'm sure it's not comfortable. His hands drop to his sides, fingers twitching. I'm sure he has another knife on him. Or a gun. Neither will do him any good.

My free hand lands on his shoulder, and he jolts. I force him to his knees, and he knocks over the stand. It clatters into another, creating a wretched noise, and I grit my teeth.

"Confess. Then beg her for mercy," I snarl.

"I'd rather he didn't beg. It's distasteful in these situations."

The way she says it, coupled with the smirk on her lips, tells me all I need to know. I file the information away for later.

"How many women have you forced yourself upon?" I snap, suddenly wanting to get this over with.

I grip his ridiculously coiffed hair and yank his head back. Disgust swirls through his eyes, hatred stamped on his face. Too bad he won't be able to funnel his rage into anything but dying.

"You think you're tough because you snuck up on me? You couldn't take me in a fair fight."

I roll my eyes, glancing at Melody. "I fear we're not going to be able to force this information from him, Melody. Perhaps we should just skip to the torture?"

She giggles, hiding her grin behind her small hand, then looks away. Chad snarls as if he has the right to be personally offended by our banter. He doesn't own her, and I'll make sure he knows that before the light leaves his eyes.

"Something amiss, prick?" He doesn't deserve for me to use his name.

Chad sniffs, attempting to put distance between his skin and my blade. "She won't give in to you. She's a fucking prude. She'll lead you on, all while acting like a goddamn slut. Then she'll reject you. I don't know what she's told you—"

"Pity I was there to witness many of your transgressions. I was there when you admitted to stalking her. I was there to hear you dismiss her rejection and threaten her. I know all about men like you." I lean down to whisper in his ear. "You touched what was mine. And now you'll pay with your blood."

He blanches, his eyes darting to Melody as if she'll save him. She crosses her arms under her magnificently presented tits. She doesn't even realize what a vision she is. An avenging angel here to exact justice through my hand.

"Melody, please. I'm sorry. I'm a nice guy. I only said those things because I thought it's what you wanted." He folds his hand together in supplication.

I whip my knife away and kick him in the back. He topples to his hands and knees, wheezing. I seize his hair again and force him upright as he struggles for breath.

"You do not address her. You do not look at her. You are dirt beneath her feet and will know your place." My harsh voice echoes around the hall.

I glance at Melody to gauge her reaction. I'd rather not frighten her, but I will not allow him to disrespect her. Instead of terror, her eyes blaze with desire. She stares at me and her lips part. When her tongue darts out, I swallow a groan.

Leaning down, I grip his chin and force his head up. "You see her? How much she craves me? *That* is something you will never experience, especially with her."

I straighten and heave him to his feet. He stumbles, almost throwing me off balance. I growl, but he doesn't stop wobbling around like a newborn calf finding its legs for the first time. When he swings around, I'm ready for him. Blocking his blow is easy. His kick glances off my shin. If he were anyone else, I'd admire his efforts.

He sneers, his lip curling as he faces me and lifts his fists. I slip my knife into its sheath, then wait for his next move. Melody clears her throat, and I glance at her. Concern lines her eyes and I smile.

She flings her hand out, a cry of warning leaving her. Again, I'm ready for him and I swat his arm away. Blood sprays from his nose as I bury my fist into his face. Flinging his hands to his nose, he stumbles back. It only takes a swift kick from me, and he tumbles off the riser. He knocks over several chairs and his head bounces on the hard floor.

Contrary to the wood of the stage, the orchestra pit is lined with concrete for acoustic purposes. I'm sure he'll be dazed if he's able to get to his feet at all. He rolls, still clutching his nose.

I jump down next to him, then swiftly kick him in the side. His ribs give easily under the toe of my boot. I grin in satisfaction and do it again. His body curls into a ball and I swear he's sobbing. I punch him in the ear, though the angle leaves something to be desired.

"Xavier?" Melody's voice rings through my bloodlust, and I pull in a deep breath before looking at her.

"Yes, Melody?"

"I don't mean to interrupt your fun, but could I borrow your knife?" She gives me an innocent smile and shrugs.

I chuckle, kicking Chad one last time, then unbuckle my sheath. "Of course, my sweet. Would you like me to bring him up to you?"

Her nose wrinkles as she glances at her feet. "No. I'd rather not get blood on the stage. It would be hard to get the stains out."

She saunters her way to the stairs and elegantly descends them, the corner of her dress gripped in her hand. When she approaches the timpani, she examines one after another. Finally, she looks up and nods.

"Where would you like him?" I ask, gesturing with my chin at the man still cowering at my feet.

"Do you think he'll run? Perhaps you should bring him over here, so we don't have to chase after him. Wouldn't want to waste any more of our night, would we?"

Whoever this ravishing creature is, I'm not entirely sure. I sensed Melody's darker side when I was trapped in the xylophone, but it runs so much deeper than I expected.

Perhaps I'm rubbing off on her. Or maybe this is who she truly is, and she's merely never had the chance to explore. Within my world, she's free to do what she likes with no reprisal. I'll indulge her every whim.

Seizing Chad, I drag him through the rows, kicking chairs and music stands out of my way. Rounding the timpani, I have the urge to throw his body against the wall, yet refrain. I hand her the knife, my fingers closing over hers, and her lip sneaks between her teeth once again.

I drop the prick and loop my arm around her waist to tug her close. "You keep that up and you'll end up with your skirts over your head again before we've taken care of him."

Chapter Eleven

Melody

Xavier's words resonate through me as he kisses me soundly. He releases me just as quickly and prowls back to Chad. My grip tightens on the knife, and a flash of anxiety streaks through my chest until I remind myself there's a cover on the blade.

I'm not even remotely trained to wield a weapon, even one like this. It's heavier than I expected, the handle intricately carved. I turn it over, noting the repetitive pattern. It's familiar, plucking at a memory long forgotten.

"Fucking whore," Chad screams at me, and my head whips up.

Xavier takes care of Chad by slamming his fist into the side of my stalker's head. He shakes his head before baring his teeth at Xavier. Chad doesn't seem able to keep his damn mouth shut. Rage swirls through me and I rip the sheath from the blade.

Stalking to the largest of the four timpani drums, I sink the tip into the top. Should I be defacing an instrument, especially one so old? No. Do I care? Not one fucking bit. The knife easily cuts through the skin.

Chad curses behind me, yet I continue. One by one, I hack

the instruments apart until they're nothing but strips of skin hanging dejectedly inside the copper drums.

Spinning around, I can barely contain myself. I bounce on the balls of my feet, waiting for Xavier to finish his assault on the other man. I don't know what's come over me, but I'm not complaining.

The more Chad screams, the giddier I become. Chad is paying for the sins of every man who's ever hurt me. For every man who harassed me. For every man who thought they were owed something merely because they had a dick. And I refuse to feel bad about it.

"Xavier, could we move this along?" As much as this heals a part of me, I still want my answers from him.

He scowls, turning blazing eyes to me. "Can't have it both ways, Melody. You wanted him to suffer, so suffer he will."

He aims another kick at Chad's side. I barely recognize the man who was threatening me not long ago. His eyes are swollen shut, blood seeping from his ears and nose. I should be queasy and ready to toss my cookies. For some reason, I'm not. Maybe something really is broken inside of me. This could be Xavier's influence, but honestly, it's probably me.

I jolt from my thoughts as Xavier's fingers wrap around mine. He pries the blade from my numb fingers, then slides it back into the sheath. My eyes track his movements and fixate on the red splattered across his knuckles. It's not blood, thank fuck. I don't want any part of Chad near me.

I twitch when that same hand tucks my hair behind my ear, and I meet his eyes. He tilts his head, studying my face. Apparently, he doesn't find what he's searching for. He tugs me away from a moaning Chad, stopping when we reach my xylophone.

I stare at the instrument, expecting the ever-present pull. Yet nothing comes. It's just another piece in this empty hall. I sigh, wondering if I lost it. Maybe giving into that dark beast within me has severed any connection I once had.

I don't know how I'll survive without music in my life. It's been the one constant since I was young. It saved me when my parents fought. It kept me going when I was rejected over and over. It was all I had for a long time. It's still all I have. I can't lose music too.

"If you want to retreat, you may," Xavier murmurs, brushing his fingers along my jaw. "There's no shame in knowing your limits, Melody."

"I'm not upset about...*that*." I wave my hand toward Chad, disgust making my nose wrinkle.

He cups my cheeks, resting his forehead against mine. "Then tell me what it is."

"Maybe we should just call the police," I whisper, closing my eyes. It's not what I wanted to say, but opening up to a man I just met doesn't seem wise.

"That's not your fear."

I snort, attempting to turn away, but he stops me. "How could you possibly know that?"

"Because we're kindred spirits, brought together against all odds. Push aside your insecurities and give in to the feelings within you. Do you honestly believe I don't know you? Are you convinced we're not destined?" He leans back to study me properly.

"We don't even know each other."

He smirks as he trails a finger down my neck and across my collarbone. "Are you sure about that?"

He drops his hands and stalks back to Chad. Every time he focuses on me, I'm swept up in the feelings. I like to think I have common sense. Nothing about what I've done tonight screams smart or healthy.

The shit he spews should be just that—shit. Yet he sounds perfectly sane while he's saying it. And I gobble it down like it's the most sensible thing in the world. Shaking my head, I wonder what the hell I'm going to do when the sun rises.

"The bitch deserved it," Chad spits out, and my stomach flips.

"Perhaps you'd like to elaborate?" Xavier leans against the large timpani.

He twirls his knife as if he has not a care in the world. I had grand plans of gutting the timpani, then Chad. Being waylaid by my own inhibitions wasn't on the schedule. I'm in no position to stab another person. I'd probably hurt myself and ruin the night. The more filth that tumbles from Chad's bloody lips, the more I wish I would have kept the blade.

Chad blathers on about deserving a woman's attention and none of them knew how good they had it until he took their control away. He's barely able to get the words out he's speaking so quickly, trying to sway Xavier to his cause. I wonder how many women he's hurt. Doesn't matter. He won't be able to do it again.

Xavier glances up, and I'm caught in his eyes. I don't know what my face is doing, but he nods. I thought this was what I wanted. I *told* him it's what I wanted. Now I just want it to be over.

The longer Chad talks, the more I want him to shut up. His thick voice wheezing out of his swollen throat grates on my nerves. I swear there's spiders crawling across my skin. Or maybe it's tiny lightning bolts electrifying my body. Either way, I want out. Closing my eyes, a shudder runs through me.

Abruptly, the noise cuts out. When I open my eyes again, Xavier has his fancy tie stuffed in Chad's mouth and he's dragging him toward the timpani. Chad lets out a muffled scream as he hauls him inside the open drum.

"I had an elaborate plan laid out for you, prick. However, we'll have to cut this short. My girl needs my attention. You understand."

I tilt my head as I bite my lip. "Um, Xavier? I don't think he's going to fit in there?"

His head whips toward me, shock flitting across his features. It's gone as quickly as it came, and he smirks.

"I shall make him fit, have no fear." A second later a crack echoes through the air, and I wince as Chad screams behind his gag.

"I'm just going to..." I wave my hand around, concentrating on not puking all over the xylophone as another snap punctuates the silence.

The next second Xavier is in front of me, grabbing my hand and leading me toward the stage. Chad flops around, his arm at an unnatural angle as he attempts to push himself from the timpani. I didn't even realize Xavier shoved him in there.

In any other circumstance, it'd be a hilarious sight with his ass stuffed in the bottom of the barrel and him flailing about. With the blood splatter and Chad's swollen face, it's not nearly as funny.

Xavier blocks my view and relief floods my veins. I don't know how much more I could handle watching that, no matter how much Chad deserves it. When we reach center stage, his hands wrap around my waist, and he lifts me effortlessly.

"I'll be right back for you, Melody. Please do not wander off. As much as I'd enjoy chasing you under other circumstances, I'd rather you not be traumatized by it."

I nod absentmindedly, my gaze wandering back to Chad who's desperately trying to heave himself out of the timpani. Xavier has already walked away by the time his words process.

His statement should terrify me, especially after Chad's threats. Instead, a delicious thrill climbs up my spine. Being chased through a theatre might not be so bad as long as it's with Xavier. Especially if there's a reward at the end. Xavier never did give me the punishment he talked about before. Maybe he forgot, though that doesn't seem likely.

Kicking my feet back and forth, I try to ignore the gurgling noise coming from Chad. I've spent months in the orchestra pit, but the view from the stage reveals a whole new picture. I didn't think there would be that much of a difference, since the pit isn't as sunken as others I've played in. Yet the light hits differently. The seats march off into the darkness, highlighting how empty it truly is here. If Chad had caught me alone...I shudder at the thought.

I wince as another crack rings through the silence, followed by a screaming curse from Chad. I could hop down, wander backstage, and shield myself from the pain Xavier is inflicting, but seeing this through feels like something I should do.

A flash of light off Xavier's blade catches my eye. The distance makes what he's doing feel surreal, as if I'm watching a show. My stomach settles and I stare while he systematically dismantles Chad. First, he cuts each ankle, the edge gliding through the tendon as easily as it did the skin of the timpani. Chad's arm swings wildly at him, making it easy for Xavier to seize his wrist and slice it open. I turn away when he grabs Chad's other hand.

Stifled sobs take over as his blood slowly gathers under his body. "Xavier? Could he bleed enough to drown in his own blood before he passed out from blood loss?"

"I suspect not. We can always make the attempt, though." He smiles, his dark eyes twinkling. "For science, of course."

"Of course." I grin. "But I'd rather not listen to his bellyaching while we're experimenting."

"Would you like me to remove his voice box? It's just a few slices to sever the cords." He dangles the blade above Chad's throat as the other man screams through his gag. It seems to be the only thing he can do now that he's incapacitated.

"Do whatever you think is best. I'm leaving in five minutes, whether you're done or not." I bite my lip as I swing my feet back and forth again.

He sucks in a breath and drops the knife. The tip sticks into Chad's Adam's apple and I grimace. Xavier grabs the handle, digging it deeper before wrenching it out. The coughing that ensues is almost too much, but I manage to compose myself.

"Melody?" Xavier calls, concern lacing his tone.

"I'm fine," I croak.

The nausea comes in waves. It's not even true queasiness.

Some deep-seated revulsion surfaces within me, and I realize it's Chad's presence. He truly does represent every vile creature I've ever encountered. And while I'm thankful he's being held accountable, it doesn't mean the problem is gone. Killing Chad doesn't eradicate the threat. There will always be another Chad to take his place. It's a depressing thought, but it doesn't make it untrue.

Xavier appears before me, and I blink slowly at him. His hands land on my upper thighs. With me sitting on the stage, he has to look up at me. Something itches at the back of my mind. It's not until his lip twitches I realize what it is.

"Where's the blood?" None on his face, his neck, his hands. Even his clothes are as pristine as they were before.

"Blood doesn't stain me if it's tainted," he murmurs as his fingers massage my legs.

"I...I don't know what that means." As much as I'd prefer him to keep running his hands along my body, I really do need answers.

He sighs, reading the determination on my face. "What are the chances you'll allow me to bury my face between your legs before I tell you?"

I roll my eyes, sitting back on my hands. "Close to zero. Tell me what the hell is going on."

"Would you perhaps like to retire away from his muffled moaning? No? Fine." He strides away from the stage only to come right back, stepping between my legs. "I am not from...this time. I've been cursed to stay within this theatre."

He's hiding something, but I can't figure out what. Maybe he's married. Or a scammer.

Oh shit.

Maybe he really is a serial killer. And I just led his latest victim right into his hands. Except I can't muster any regret for Chad. He deserved what was coming to him.

"How'd you do the music? It didn't sound like it was coming from speakers." I glance around the space. Even now I can't find them. The PA system is another one of those old features from way back when.

He cocks his head, confusion flooding his face. "What speakers? No one is here but us."

I narrow my eyes, trying to figure out if he's playing a part or really doesn't know what speakers are. I slip my phone from my pocket and pull up a search engine.

"Xavier Sebastian Cantrell, right?" I type in the name, then peer at him.

"The third. What are you doing?"

"I'm searching you." I flash the screen at him and hit enter.

Articles from hundreds of years ago pop up, discussing the opening of a theatre—this theatre. Apparently, it was a big to-do, if this is any indication. And the owner, some pompous ass who allegedly sullied many unmarried ladies, was none other than Xavier Sebastian Cantrell the Third.

"You were kind of a manwhore, huh?"

Chapter Twelve

Xavier

Scowling, I duck my head again. I don't know what Melody has in her hand, but it seems to have accessed my past. I'd rather have introduced her to my sowing oats days later, once I explained the curse. Alas, I suppose I'll have to endure whatever jesting she has in store for me. At least there's glee stamped across her face instead of horror.

"They were all willing participants in the rendezvous. If their fathers didn't approve, well, that could not be helped," I say delicately, and she snorts. "Shall we get on with what has happened since?"

I'm suddenly very keen to tell her of the curse, if only to turn her away from my nefarious past. I did nothing wrong, but I'd rather not discuss my conquests with Melody. She is all that matters now. She waves her hand for me to continue, grinning, though her eyes keep darting to the device in her hands.

"Shortly after I purchased this theatre, I ran into a spot of trouble." How the fuck am I supposed to explain this? "After a few years, and more than a couple mistakes, I was arrogant. Pompous, as you say. I knew I needed to focus, but I was too late."

She tilts her head, gazing at me. "What does that mean?"

At least she isn't immediately dismissing everything I'm saying. She might just believe me if I can adequately portray what really happened. It was a long time ago, though. The details aren't as clear as they once were.

"I should have been concentrating on how to bring music to the masses. How to expand the business. Instead, I was set on blazing my way through the world. I was gone too much and when I was here, I was distracted and disorganized. And then there was the fire. It only burned the back of the theatre, but it spread quickly. Panic ensued with a full house." I sigh, running my hands through my hair as the memories of that night flit through my brain. "Instead of restoring order and saving what I could, I retreated to the tunnels below."

She straightens, brows pulling low over her eyes. "Wait, there really is a tunnel system underground? Like in *Phantom of the Opera?*"

"I don't know what that is, but what you described to the prick, yes. There's an escape route down there. We built it in case a husband randomly popped up. Or if society fell."

"We?"

I glance away, swallowing hard. "I had a business partner. And friend. He begged me to help him get the people out. I refused, saying I would save myself. It was selfish, I see that now. However, once the fire spread, I was trapped. An invisible barrier kept me from escaping. And he was there, waiting for me when I came back. The fire was out, but he cursed me soundly for my transgressions."

She tips her chin up and narrows her eyes. "As he should have. I assume people died? And you didn't care?"

"I did, just not soon enough. My arrogance was rampant, and it became my downfall. Regret has not helped me in the ensuing years. I spent a long time blaming him for my circumstances. Once I came to terms with my own complacency, I thought the curse would break. But the cycle started once more until I finally accepted my fate."

"Wait, what fate?" She glances at the phone. "It says Xavier died in that fire. Are you, like, his great-great-great-grandson or something?"

My mouth twitches, though there's nothing funny about her question. "I told you who I was, Melody. When I say he cursed me, he wasn't throwing harsh words at my feet. He was literally cursing me—to reside in the place I abandoned. To rot while I watched my beautiful theatre exchange hands over and over with no input from me. To wallow as patron after patron came to experience the beauty I had so ruthlessly thrown away."

Her sharp burst of laughter stings my skin and stabs my heart. I didn't expect her to believe it outright, but to laugh at my pain hurts in a way I never expected. If she can't grasp the truth of the curse, I fear she won't accept the rest. Telling her I've been residing in her xylophone while she plays will tip her over the edge. I'm sure of it.

"Sorry. It's just...people don't get cursed. I mean, not like this. Sure, I could be open to believing someone could have someone wish them harm. And I'm not totally convinced ghosts are a figment of people's imaginations, but this is a bit far-fetched, don't you think? I mean, someone would have noticed you skulking around."

"They would were I corporeal," I mutter.

"I'm sorry. Did you just suggest that I'm the only one who can see you? Because that's...that's not...Chad." She flings her hand out toward the now-silent man stuffed in the timpani. He died without us noticing—no witnesses to mourn him. As it should be.

I pull in a deep breath, steeling myself. "It was the final performance tonight. No one stays late these nights. If they did, they would have seen me as well."

"So, you just hide in your attic? Or roam the tunnels? You're going to have to do better than—"

"I'm trapped within the xylophone the rest of the time." I

blurt out the words without thought. Her insistence I must be lying wears on my nerves and my muscles tighten.

Her lips part as if she'll refute my claim. A pensive look overtakes her face and her eyes stare into nothing. A minute passes as she works through what I've said. While curses weren't commonplace in my time, I gather they're even less regarded now. Perhaps her hesitancy has nothing to do with me and everything to do with the world outside these walls.

"The pull. The connection you talked about," she finally whispers, her gaze still fixed on a far-off point.

"You felt it too, whether you want to admit it or not."

She waves her hand listlessly, batting away my statement. "I'm past that. I've moved on to the fact I felt it when I played."

I step closer, placing my hands on either side of her hips. She doesn't seem to notice as her legs widen, allowing me to ease my body between them. I'd touch her, but I'm afraid it will break whatever spell she's under.

"You felt it when you *weren't* playing as well. It haunted your dreams, lured you through the city, called your name upon the song of the wind. It filled you up and healed your soul," I murmur as I brush my thumb along her thighs through the fabric of her dress.

"How did you know?" she breathes, her eyes finding mine.

I smile. Not the alluring tip of my lips from before. This is genuine—real. "Because I feel it too."

"Did you really get cursed? And how did we connect if you did?"

"Yes, I did. I could point to a million ways to test it, but most of them are uncomfortable. And I'd rather spend the time with you. Preferably inside your beautiful cunt." My smile morphs into the smirk I tried so hard to keep under control.

She scoffs and rolls her eyes. "You made big promises the last time, and while I might have orgasmed while you were fingering me, the rest was definitely not the masterpiece you claimed it would be."

Fear, or maybe shame, flashes across her face, and she bites her lip. My hands circle her waist and her palms slap against the stage as she sits back. A shudder runs through her, though she tries to stop it. Desire flames in her eyes and her breasts heave against her bodice as she pulls in a deep breath. The effect I have on her is intoxicating, and my cock hardens.

"If you would have listened, it would have been more. Don't think I forgot about your need for punishment. You disobeyed me."

She gasps as I run my hands down her legs. "How the hell did I do that?"

"You didn't wait for the crescendo. Are you going to sit back and take your punishment like a good girl?"

Her wide eyes find mine, and she nods as her chin trembles. I smirk one more time before I dip my head under her skirts. A soft *oh* escapes her when I lick my way from her knee to her inner thigh. Her legs tremble when I repeat the move on the other side. Sinking my teeth into her flesh, I revel in the delicious noises falling from her lips. I do it again, just to hear her moan.

"Xavier," she groans as I slide her closer to the edge of the stage until her ass practically hangs off.

I guide her legs over my shoulder and bury my nose into her sweet cunt, inhaling deeply. A shudder rolls through me. Utterly intoxicating. Her scent alone could pull me under, drowning me in its seductive aroma.

My tongue darts out, licking her from core to clit, and I groan, tilting my head back. As much as I want to spend the rest of my night under her skirts, a trickle of sweat drips down my neck. I flip the layers up, shoving them to her waist, and she gives me a look.

"Was that all?" she asks haughtily, raising one elegant eyebrow.

"Certainly not. Unless you'd prefer me to pass out from the heat. As much as I enjoy you in this dress, I cannot abide the skirts." I grip her thighs, digging my fingers in until she gasps. "Lie back, and I'll continue."

She sighs as she drops and folds her hands over her stomach. She stares at the ceiling and my nostrils flare. I didn't realize what a little brat she would be. A thrill rolls through me at the thought.

"Careful, little muse," I murmur into her thigh before biting her again. My marks from before have faded, leaving the desire to make them permanent. I growl, then lap at the redness, dipping my tongue into the grooves.

"Did you bite me?" she cries, but her words waver, a breathlessness taking over her voice.

"I certainly did. I'd tattoo my marks onto your skin if I could, inking my essence into your very being. You'd carry me with you forever, never failing in your devotion to me."

I don't give her time to answer, especially since I'm afraid of how she'll respond. Instead, I lick her soaked cunt, gathering her essence on my tongue. I've never tasted anything as sweet. She whimpers, sliding her fingers into my hair. As she grips the strands, a delicious burn slices through my scalp.

I devour her, swirling around her clit before retreating to her core. The longer I drag out her pleasure, the harder she tugs. I slip one finger inside her cunt and pump in and out slowly. Her muscles coil tighter when I add another, and I grin. Sucking on that sensitive bud, I thrust into her. Her legs tremble before snapping around my head, trapping me between her thighs.

I ease my mouth away and bury my fingers deep inside. Her cry of frustration echoes through the space, and I chuckle against her flesh. I can't help but lick her again as I drop my hand from her.

"What the fuck?" she whines, and her hands fall to her sides, slapping against the stage.

"Something the matter, my sweet?" I press a kiss to her flesh, right above her clit.

"I was almost there and you dropped the ball. Again." Annoyance laces her tone.

I snicker as I glance up. Her eyes widen as our gazes meet, and a flush splashes across her cheeks. She really is the most exquisite creature I've ever met.

"I haven't even begun. Once you learn to follow directions, you'll be allowed to come. Beg for me and I'll consider it."

I nuzzle her cunt, then begin again. Her protests die on her tongue as I build her up once more. Her hands return and so do mine. Each time her pussy quivers around my fingers, I curl them. And each time I retreat just before she can tumble into oblivion. She squirms and I throw my arm over her waist to keep her still.

"Please," she cries out. "Please make me come."

"Perfect," I mumble against her flesh.

Another cry of protest leaves her when I step away completely. She props herself onto her elbows, confusion mixed with annoyance stamped across her face. I lick my lips, then my fingers, savoring the taste of her. If I'm lucky, her scent will cling to me the rest of the night.

Tucking my hands under her ass, I knead the flesh before settling her more firmly on the stage. I gather the layers of her skirt, securing them under her. The thought of her basking in the glow of the spotlight with her cunt on full display sends a throbbing ache to my cock.

When I pivot, a noise of protest echoes through the theatre. "Where the hell do you think you're going?"

I glance over my shoulder and run my gaze along her body. Cheeks blushing a deep red. Tits heaving against her neckline. Legs dangling over the rim of the stage. And that beautifully soaked cunt, quivering as it leaks onto the dark wood beneath her. I've never seen such a masterpiece.

"Your begging has inspired me. However, I require a little... assistance for what I have in store to reward you. I beg only a moment, Melody. Perhaps you'd like to touch yourself while I'm away?" I raise an eyebrow as her mouth parts and she nods. "You may do so, but you will not come. Not unless it's by my hand, my mouth, my cock. Understood?"

Another nod and I turn again to skirt around the timpani

where Chad's cooling body resides. I barely afford him a glance. The world is a better place without him in it. Her bag sits next to the xylophone, and my fingers itch to grab it and run back to her. I keep my gait steady, though. I can feel her gaze tracking me from the stage, wondering what I'm up to.

Struggling to get into the top, I finally get it open and snatch the items I need, a thrill running through me as I do. When I stand and make my way toward her once more, my feet stutter to a stop.

She's rested her feet on the edge of the stage, knees bent and skirts billowing around her middle. The spotlight hits her pretty cunt at just the right angle, along with her hand sliding along her folds. I'm tempted to pull my cock out to relieve the need building within me. Stroking myself won't be nearly as satisfying as fucking her, but to come while she pleasures herself ignites a fire within me.

I stalk back to her, my eyes fixed between her legs. As I reach her, I lean down and suck her clit in my mouth, and she yelps. Releasing the small bud, I lick her once more before straightening. When she attempts to pull her hand away, I latch onto her wrist, silently encouraging her to continue. Her back arches and I use my grip to guide her movements as she thrusts her fingers into her core.

When her legs begin to shake, I drag her hand away, then pop her fingers in my mouth. Her ass bounces as she whimpers, and her feet slip from the stage to dangle once more. When I've sufficiently cleaned her skin, I place her palm next to her hip.

"Feet on the stage, Melody."

Her legs practically fly over her head as she rushes to comply. Her eagerness is a balm to my soul, and a note of desire reverberates through my heart.

"Please, Xavier. I need more," she pleads.

"Anything for you, my sweet little muse. Tell me, Melody. Do you trust me?" I slide my present for her along her inner thigh.

She props herself up again and peeks over her voluptuous skirts. "Are those my mallets?"

"Indeed they are. Your practice ones, of course. I noticed you cleaned them thoroughly, as you should. However, you didn't answer my question," I murmur, then slide the head along around her clit.

Her eyes glaze over and she pants while I play with her. "What are you going to do with them?"

I grind the rubber head against her clit, then slide it down to her core, resting it there. "Do. You. Trust. Me."

It's a demand now. If she refuses, I'll have to abandon my plans and come up with something else. If she'll even let me.

"Yes," she breathes, her back arching off the stage.

I slip the mallet halfway into her soaking cunt, and her hips buck, attempting to pull it deeper. The rubber slides easily with the help of her wetness, and I twirl the handle. I wish I could swallow the delicious noises falling from her lips, but that will have to wait until I'm buried inside her instead.

"More," she moans, and I push the head fully inside.

Ducking my head, I hum against her clit and twist the mallet handle. I lick and suck on the small bud until she's writhing under my ministrations. Before long, she sails over the edge, my name a sob upon her lips. I draw out her pleasure, squeezing every last drop of ecstasy from her body. Her legs slide from my shoulders as she pants.

Straightening, I survey her body—chest heaving, skin damp and shimmering, dark eyes glazed with desire. This is what I was missing all these years I've been locked away. Pausing to gaze at her trembling form, I wonder how far I can push her. Where do her boundaries truly lie?

I grip her wrist and tug her upright. She protests but does my silent bidding. Blinking at me slowly, she slips her lip between her teeth, and I smirk. I twirl the mallet, still buried deep within her, and she gasps as her head tips back. I pull it from her gradually. Gripping her chin, I force her to look at me.

"Open," I growl and use my thumb to force her lips to part.

I slip the mallet, soaked with her desire, into her mouth. Her tongue swirls around the piece, and my cock strains against my pants. Her eyes lock with mine as her cheeks hollow while she sucks on it, tasting herself just as I have.

"Before this night is through, you'll be on your knees, using that tongue in the way it was intended."

Chapter Thirteen

Melody

I'm still reeling from the multitude of emotions flowing through me. I'm not convinced Xavier's telling me the truth about who he is, even with the evidence on my phone. Maybe he completely assumed someone's identity, thinking it was a cool tale.

Then again, the connection I've felt from the xylophone certainly resonates from him. I assumed it was a sign I was where I belong, but now I'm second-guessing myself.

He keeps glancing back at me as he pulls me through the stairwells to his attic room. I'm sure he assumes I'm freaked out. Curses aren't exactly accepted lore these days. I never gave it much thought until now, but the more I mull it over, the less concerned I am.

I wonder if he's more worried with the fact he just put my practice mallets in a place they definitely weren't designed to go. I can't stop the grin from spreading across my face.

My sexual exploits have never been very exciting. Xavier pushing my limits exhilarates me. I'm practically skipping with anticipation to see what he comes up with next.

I'm barely paying attention to where he's taking me, trusting he won't lead me astray. Clearly, I trust him with my body. Plus, he already killed Chad for me.

"What are we going to do about the body?" I ask as I trip up the stairs.

He swings around and hauls my body into his. I gasp, my hands landing on his hard chest. His muscles bunch, flexing under my palms as he steadies us.

"The only body I'm concerned with is the one you're hiding under this dress," he murmurs, then kisses me hard and fast before releasing me.

We continue our journey, the darkness deepening with every turn. None of this looks familiar. Then again, I wasn't exactly worried about the decorations on the walls when he was bringing me here the first time. I was too pissed off at the disappointing conclusion of our little rendezvous. He certainly made up for it on the stage, but I need more. My body is practically vibrating with need. I don't know if he notices.

"We really should figure out how to get him out of the timpani at the very least," I snap, hitching up my skirts a little more.

"We really don't. It'll be taken care of by dawn."

We reach the last landing, his bedroom door coming into view. "Okay, but how? Because I really think it's something we should—"

He spins me around and my back thuds against the wood, the handle rattling. His hands land on either side of my head, and he presses his body into mine. My breath catches in my throat as pinpricks of desire prickle my skin. His knee shoves between my thighs, and the wetness between my legs soaks into the layers of skirts separating us.

"When I tell you not to worry about it, you leave it be, Melody. You trust that I have it taken care of. Understood?" He raises an eyebrow.

I nod, biting my tongue to keep my questions inside. He

doesn't seem convinced, but he ducks his head and nuzzles my neck. I tilt my head and my eyes flutter shut. I let go of the worries plaguing my mind, giving myself over to the sensations running rampant through my body.

His teeth sink into my flesh, probably leaving a mark, not that I care. He wants me to have something to remember him by, if only for a while. My heart aches at the thought, though I don't fully understand why. It's not like I can fall for someone in the course of one night.

His lips brush across my skin until he seals his mouth over mine. His tongue sweeps across my own and a shudder runs through me. He pushes back, leaving me bereft.

His ever-present smirk appears as he tugs me away from the door, then swings it open. When he releases me, a chill skates down my spine. Tipping his chin, he gestures for me to get inside, and I step backward.

"On the bed, little vixen," he growls.

I swallow hard and shuffle back until my calves hit the massive bed. I sink onto the mattress, holding back an audible groan. It's fluffy, like resting on a cloud. Even the four large posts holding up the canopy have flowing curtains wrapped around them. I've never experienced a bed so incredibly comfortable. I fling out my arms and fall back. My eyes close and I sigh, a smile blooming across my face.

"Comfortable?" he murmurs, and my eyes fly open. I didn't expect him to be so close.

"Where did you get this bed? It's fucking heaven." I wiggle around, sinking further into the comforter. I swear it's made of fluffy marshmallows.

His face sobers before he glances away. "Just showed up. Doesn't matter. We have other business to attend to."

He stalks away to his wall of masks. The collection is ridiculous and amazing all at once. I wonder if they "just showed up" too.

If he actually is from the past, I wouldn't be surprised to find he personally curated each of them himself. He snatches one and pivots before prowling back to me.

He drops his knee between my legs, and I slide toward him as the mattress sinks under his weight. I'm trapped by my skirts, but I'm not complaining. The closer he is to me, the calmer I feel. It's like all my questions vanish in the wake of his presence. I should be worried about that, except his scent invades my senses, distracting me once again with its woody undertones. Everything about him infiltrates my mind, shoving my fears aside.

"Sit up," he commands, and my body obeys without thought.

Balancing on my elbows, I wait for his next move. He slips the mask's ties behind my head, securing them before sliding it over my eyes. I didn't realize I wouldn't be able to see at all.

His weight disappears, and I'm left to whip my head from side to side, attempting to track his movements. I reach up to remove the fabric and his fingers seize my wrist.

"Leave it and stand up." There's a gruffness in his voice that wasn't there a minute ago.

Sighing, I shove to my feet. I hide my fingers in the layers of my dress, clutching the fabric tightly. Anticipation rolls through me, my other senses heightened. When his fingers brush across my neck, gathering my hair and tying it back, I bite my cheek to keep my moan inside. No reason he needs to know how needy I am.

His breath ghosts across the shell of my ear before he whispers, "Did I tell you to keep quiet? Don't hide your pleasure from me."

He slowly undresses me, yanking my body around according to his whims. As the dress falls around my ankles, he gathers up my hand and I step out. He drops his hold on me, and I lick my lips. The rustle of fabric barely covers his sharp inhale.

"On the bed, Melody. You're going to put on a little show."

I turn my head toward the sound of something being dragged across the floor. I shiver, though not from the cold. In fact, it's warm up here, tucked away from the rest of the world. Here, anything could happen.

I've never given up my control. I've never allowed myself to indulge in some of the fantasies I've had over the years. Not that I had many people to explore with. I've always felt a little outside of society, as if I was born in the wrong time. Maybe Xavier was right and we were destined to find each other.

Making up my mind, I scramble onto the soft bed. My body thrums with anticipation of his next move. I don't know what he expects and after a full minute, I'm almost afraid to ask.

Doubt seeps in, wondering if he's left me here—blindfolded and naked. What a humiliation that would be. At least there's no one else to witness my embarrassment. I open my mouth to finally say something, anything, and he hums. The sound rumbles in my chest and heat gathers between my legs.

"Cup your breasts and play with your nipples. Make them hard for me, just as you do my cock."

Another shot of lust spears into me. Goosebumps pebble along my skin as I slide my hands to my breasts. My thumbs brush over the already hard nubs and I whimper. Back and forth, again and again. I imagine his eyes fixed on me and my breathing becomes erratic. I roll them between my fingers, plucking at them until I'm practically bowing off the bed. Usually, this wouldn't have such an effect on me, but knowing he's watching creates a firestorm within me.

I suck in a deep breath when something brushes against my leg. I'm convinced it's Xavier, but a second later I realize it's just the sheets. My hands stall as thoughts tumble from my mind. Not knowing what he's doing, where he is, if he's left me...all of it leaves me numb. I'm lost in a sea of darkness.

"What's the matter, my sweet? Would you like to stop?" Concern lines his voice and his finger skims along the arch of my foot, causing my toes to curl.

"No. I just didn't know where you were." I try to keep my tone even, but it doesn't work.

"Would you like to peek? Then you can continue with your performance," he murmurs as his finger continues skimming along my foot.

I reach up, hesitating for a split second before I lift the mask and peer out the bottom. Xavier raises an eyebrow as he leans back and rests his hands on the arms of his chair. That must be what he was dragging over. His knees practically touch the mattress, inches from my feet. If I open my legs, he'll have a clear view of, well, everything. My cheeks heat and he smirks.

"Ready to resume? I'd like to see just how far that flush travels down your beautiful body. Does your cunt blush as well, I wonder?"

He seizes my ankles, and I resist the urge to jerk away. Trusting him to take care of me is harder than I expected. I always thought of myself as too independent to allow someone else to make decisions for me. I wonder if I just never had someone I *could* trust. Even now, I'm struggling to give Xavier that kind of power. I've thrown every other inhibition out the window tonight, though. What's one more?

My muscles relax, and he pushes my feet up until my knees are bent. I let my legs fall open when he releases me, and he hums. He gestures to the mask, and I tug it down before pulling it over my face, plunging me into darkness again.

"Show me again how you touch yourself," he growls, the sound rumbling through me.

I slide my hand down my stomach and my desire roars to life once more. I close my eyes, even though I can't see through the mask. My fingers skim over the curls and he grabs my wrist, stopping my progress.

"Do not touch your cunt."

"You've got to be kidding me. This is how I touch myself." Annoyance laces my tone. I'm tempted to rip the cover from my eyes and glare at him.

"Play with your clit. I'll take care of the rest." His lips close around my fingers and his tongue swirls over the pads, wetting them thoroughly.

He lets go and grazes his palms from my inner thighs to my knees. I tremble and my hand drops between my legs. I circle my clit, gradually applying more pressure as he continues exploring my flesh. When his thumbs caress the crease by my pussy, a whimper leaves me.

"Slowly, Melody. Wouldn't want you coming before I'm ready," he murmurs.

I huff, doing as he wants. It's as if my body responds to him before my mind has caught up. With every interaction between us, I'm more convinced he was right. We're connected in some mysterious way. He slips one finger into my pussy, and I clench around him.

"Give yourself over to the ecstasy I willingly offer to you," he whispers and adds another finger. "So fucking wet for me."

He continues to murmur dirty things, almost to himself. The pleasure in me builds with each thrust of his fingers while my own rub my clit harder and faster. I bite my lip, concentrating on the sensations. As my pussy flutters around him, he slows and my orgasm spirals away. He crooks his fingers deep inside me and I gasp.

"Do you hear it?" he asks, starting his assault on my senses once more.

It's then I catch the low strains of music floating through the air. The low thrum of the strings, followed by the woodwinds easing into the cadence, have goosebumps blossoming across my skin.

His fingers plunge into me to the beat, pausing at the rests. The notes layer on top of one another, creating the symphony from before. I recognize the refrain. My hand falls away from my body, determined to wait for the crescendo this time.

He growls and his thumb presses against my clit. I shudder, arching my back. Flames lick through my veins, and I'm so close to the edge.

"Xavier, I can't," I whine, squirming under his ministrations.

"Let the music fill you," he commands before he rips his fingers away. "Just as I do."

His cock plunges into me just as the music crests, and I tumble into oblivion as cymbals crash in my ears, reverberating through my body. I spasm around him as he thrusts into me harder. His fingers dig into my hips, keeping me in his hold as I writhe underneath him.

"Such a good girl. You look so beautiful taking my cock." His voice is strained, barely heard over the symphony.

His words fill me just as much as the music. He buries his cock into me, stopping as I cry out in ecstasy. Needy sounds fall from my lips as he rolls his hips.

"Please," I breathe, latching onto his wrists.

He shushes me and grinds into me. His hands land on either side of my head, body covering mine. Desperation flows through me, and I thrash under him as his lips wrap around my nipple. I yelp when his teeth nip at the sensitive bud. He moves to the other, flicking it with his tongue. My fingers spear into his hair, holding him to my breast. He slides his arm around my waist and forces me up with him.

A weightlessness overtakes me as he cradles my body. He seals his mouth to mine and devours me as he stands. I'm so entranced by the hunger he's stirring in me, I don't notice we've moved until my back slams into the wall.

I moan as he grips my ass and plunges into me again without restraint. My legs wrap around his waist, and I squeeze his shoulders, holding on while he fucks me.

He rips his mouth away, burying his face into my neck. I moan again when his stomach hits my clit, sending a spark of pleasure through me. My pussy quivers and I throw my head against the wood. His teeth sink into my sensitive flesh, marking me as he has so many times tonight. All my doubts fall away in the wake of the completeness that envelops me.

"Sing for me," he growls, and I explode, his name a song on my lips.

He follows a moment later, sending me into another spiral. I've never experienced something as world altering as being with him. Only one thought remains as I float through the aftermath of the best orgasm I've ever had—this is only for tonight.

Chapter Fourteen

Xavier

I keep glancing over at Melody's slumbering form as I sit at my piano. The blankets have practically enveloped her, hiding her naked body from my view. It's probably for the best. Her body is too much of a temptation. I'd end up deep inside her before she'd even woken up. The thought makes me skip a note, and I groan in frustration.

Starting again, the notes float around the room as if they're living, breathing things. My eyes close as I give myself over to the piece I've been working on for the better part of a decade.

The composition started with a simple line of melody, and I spent my days trapped in the xylophone building it up. I didn't realize how significant it would be until Melody waltzed into the orchestra pit.

The minute she picked up the mallets, I knew she was the key I'd been waiting for. Having her here with me only confirmed what I already knew. We were meant to find one another.

I didn't want to let her sleep, but she's clearly not used to staying up all night like I am. When I'm in the xylophone, I'm in a suspended space. It's a void of nothingness and I'm merely floating in it. My heart aches with the knowledge that I'll have to return to that state, mourning the loss of Melody in my arms.

I give up on the piano and join her. She sighs when I climb in next to her, cuddling close to me while she sleeps. I wrap my arm around her waist and nuzzle her neck, breathing in her scent of lavender and lemon. I'm sure the lemon is from the oil she uses on the xylophone. It only endears her to me more. As if I needed another reason to love her.

The thought pulls me up short and I roll away, staring at the gauzy curtains draped overhead. Love is not a word I'm well acquainted with. I've given myself over to believing in the connection we have, understanding there is much more than a mere affinity for her.

But to equate this to love...I have removed myself so far from that word, I wouldn't know whether it was love. With Melody, though, it feels as easy as breathing. Not that I do that often these days.

I drop a kiss onto her bare shoulder and brush my hand down her side. She sighs, rolling her face toward me. Rolling her nipple between my thumb and finger, I watch in fascination as it hardens.

Her body responds to me just as I knew it would. I lean down, licking at the hard nub, then pull it into my mouth. A soft moan leaves her as I suck and move my hand to the other to give it the attention it deserves.

I graze my teeth against her flesh as I release her nipple. She whimpers and I shush her, then kiss the soft skin of her breast. I can't resist such a beautiful canvas laid out before me. Such loveliness deserves to be painted with my pleasure.

Gently, I pull back, admiring the mark I've left behind. I'm tempted to do it again, but I fear she will wake up, and I haven't even started yet. If we had the time, I'd cover her in them.

My hand skims down her side and she shivers. As I murmur nonsensical words into her flesh, I continue my journey to map each inch of her beneath my palm. Soon enough, my finger dips between her legs. Dropping my chin to my chest, I swallow down a groan. Even while she sleeps, she's fucking wet for me. As if her body knows who her pleasure belongs to.

I nudge her knees apart, giving me more access to her dripping pussy. Gradually, I sink my finger into her core, and she squirms. I add another one, and slowly pump them in and out.

When her breathing picks up, I wrap my lips around her nipple again. Playing with her body is something I'll never tire of. I lie on my side, watching her for a sign that she's waking up.

My cock hardens the longer I gaze at her, and I reach down with my free hand to grasp the base. Stroking myself while I fuck her with my fingers, I push all thoughts of our rapidly dwindling time together. I'll make the most of each minute until I'm forced back into that blasted instrument. If I can convince her to come back after the next performance, all the better.

"Xavier," she breathes, and my gaze darts back to her face.

Her eyes are still closed, lips slightly parted. Something inside me melts at her calling out to me while she sleeps. It's as if it's a private memory just for the two of us. It's one more indication of the connection between us.

Gently, I pull my fingers from her and lick them clean before easing around her. Gripping my cock, I rub it against her pussy, then spread her wetness down my shaft. Every time I slip inside her, the world becomes brighter. The tension in my body becomes lighter. The air fills with delicate tones.

I thrust deep into her pussy and her back arches. She gasps, fingers curling in the sheets. Her eyes find mine as I pull out slowly, then plunge into her again. A whimper leaves her, mixing with the notes dancing around us. No other sound can compare.

My life has been a meaningless void until she waltzed into it. I stop, our bodies fused together, and lean over her to place a gentle kiss on her lips.

"Again," she breathes, hands latching onto my neck to hold me close to her.

"Like this?" I pull from her inch by inch, then slam into her once more.

"Faster," she whines. "Harder. I need you."

I chuckle even as her words resonate through me. Gathering her body to mine, I kiss her again. I sit back, taking her with me, and she gasps into my mouth at the new angle.

"Were you just waiting for me to wake up and couldn't wait any longer?" she murmurs as she rolls her hips, and I groan.

I run my hands down her sides, then grip her ass. "This body was distracting me from composing our song."

She chuckles, a sound I've never heard from her before. I want to beg to hear it again. "Don't let me stop you from continuing."

I growl, sinking my teeth into her shoulder to leave yet another mark on her skin. It's not easy, but I manage to stand while still connected to her. The needy noises falling from her lips as she wraps her legs around me are almost my undoing. Walking to the piano, I hope the bench is wide enough for what I have planned.

Kicking one side of the bench, then the other, she chuckles again, and my heart warms a little more. I slide between the seat and the piano and sit, settling her on my lap.

"What exactly are you doing?" She leans back, raising an eyebrow as she clings to me.

"You wanted me to continue playing. I want to continue fucking you. Compromise, little muse. I'm surprised you've never heard of it. Better hold on. You'll be doing most of the work," I warn her before I slip my fingers from her skin to the keys.

She wiggles, gripping my shoulders, and I swallow another groan. No need for her to see how much she's affecting me. Not yet, anyway.

"Are you going to play?" she whispers in my ear.

I close my eyes and start to play. I miss my first note when she grinds into me. She *tsks*, then repeats the move. I set my jaw and glance at her with hooded eyes.

Gradually, I find a rhythm and so does she. It takes everything in me not to seize her hips and slam into her over and over. She seems to enjoy the effect she's having on me as she matches the pace I've set—slow and steady.

When I pick up the tempo, she does as well, and I grunt. Her pussy clamps around my cock, almost sending me over the edge, and I grit my teeth.

"Wait for the crescendo, maestro. Wouldn't want to come too early, would you?"

"If you continue to taunt me, I'll abandon your little game and make you come until you're begging me to stop." I nip at her bottom lip and miss the next note.

She freezes and smirks at me. "I think you like me being in control."

She emphasizes her words by clenching around my length, and I tip my head back. I'm tempted to start the piece over and make her wait. I don't know if I can hold off that long, though.

Instead, I begin at the last measure, and she sinks onto me once more. Glancing down, I'm caught by the sight of my cock disappearing into her in time with the downbeats. She stops during the rests, filling the silence with her moans. It's the perfect addition, creating a whole new layer to the composition.

My fingers fly across the keys as we near the climax. Her movements become erratic, and she chants my name, a song in and of itself upon her lips. My stomach tenses and I hold my breath when she spasms around me, crying out her release. I slam the cover over the keys and grip her hips. She yelps as I stand, the bench crashing across the floor.

Her ass barely fits on the fallboard, and I dig my fingers into her skin. I thrust into her hard and fast, just as she begged me to. Her orgasm rolls into another one and she throws her head back. I sink my teeth into her neck as I follow her into oblivion, stars sparking behind my lids. She shudders, clinging to me, and I to her.

As our breathing eases, I slip from her, the evidence of our escapades dripping down her thighs and onto the cover. I should clean it up, make sure the keys don't get wet. I won't. Her essence marking my instrument is a christening I'll remember in the cold years to come. Shoving the depressing thoughts from my mind, I shake my head.

I drop to my knees, and she scrambles to stop from slipping off the piano. I lap at her core, and she lets out a soft *oh*.

Pressing a kiss to one thigh and then the other, I murmur, "Wouldn't want to make a mess."

As I stand, a peculiar look overtakes her face, and she stares over my shoulder. Setting her feet on the floor, I guide her gaze back to me.

"Something the matter?"

"If you really are a guy from like way back when—"

"Which I am."

She waves away my interjection. "Can I come back?"

Desperation and hope bloom in her eyes while despair crashes into me. I don't have the answers she seeks. I've never been in this position before. No one has captured me the way she has. There was no one else I wanted, much less was able to be with.

I was lost, merely waiting for her to appear. With her here, I never want to let her leave. If I could, I would lock her away and live out my days in this theatre with only my sweet Melody. I sigh as I gaze into her beautiful blue eyes. I'd rather she wasn't witness to my disappearance into the xylophone.

"While I would assume I'll return to this form after the next final performance, I actually do not know. I've never been in this position before." I swallow hard, an ache burning through my chest.

"You've never..." She presses her lips together and blows out her cheeks.

I smirk, then drop a kiss on her forehead. "I told you before, Melody. We're meant to be. Brought together by fate. I never needed anyone else."

Chapter Fifteen

Melody

A few hours was not enough sleep, but I don't want to waste what little time we have left. I've given up trying to figure out whether or not he's telling me the truth. It doesn't matter either way.

All I know is I don't want to leave. This is the most peaceful I've felt in years, if ever. Being with him feels right. Whether it's fate or the cosmos or some curse, I don't know. And I don't particularly care. If tonight truly is all we have, I won't spend the hours lounging in his bed.

"What else is here? I want to know all the secrets of this place." I attempt to infuse my voice with an enthusiasm I don't fully feel.

"There are plenty of things I can show you right here," he says, pulling my body into his.

A shiver rolls down my spine and heat licks through my stomach. All he has to do is look at me and I'm wet again. It must be him, because I've never had this happen to me before. My experience in the bedroom has been lackluster thus far. Now I'm convinced I was hooking up with the wrong men. Or maybe it was that I wasn't hooking up with *him.*

"We can't just stay in the attic the rest of the night. And the sun will be up soon. I want to explore," I mutter even as I tilt my head to give him access to my skin.

His teeth tug at my earlobe and my eyes flutter shut. It wouldn't be so bad to stay here. We could play with more of the masks. I wouldn't be surprised if the trunk sitting in the corner of the room held an assortment of other toys, though I doubt they're the ones I'm used to.

"Would you like to see the underground tunnels?" he whispers in my ear.

"Yes," I breathe, though I've forgotten the question in the wake of his hands running over my skin.

He hums, then nips at my jaw. Suddenly, he steps back, leaving me chilled without his warmth. He turns and gathers the dress I was wearing. His brows pull low as he stares at it. I hope I didn't rip it.

Technically, it belongs to the theatre. I'd rather not get scolded because I wrecked one of their precious costumes. He tosses it in the corner and stomps to the trunk. My mouth drops open, but I snap it shut. If Xavier isn't worried, then I shouldn't be either, I suppose.

He flips back the lid and digs around for a bit before producing a white dress. It's long and flowy and noticeably missing the stays from the last garment. Relief floods me as I remember how they restricted my breathing. I could barely sit back on the stage while he...my cheeks heat and I press my palms to them. He gestures with his chin and I turn.

The fabric floats around my body. I slip my arms into the long tight sleeves that end at my elbows, then billow out and drape to my wrists. There's more lace than I normally would wear, but it fits perfectly. The front ends just below my knees, making it easy to sweep the long train around as I spin back to him. His eyes dip to my chest and he smirks. The low neckline combined with the empire waist pushes my breasts up, creating almost as much cleavage as the previous dress.

"Why does this dress feel familiar?" I ask as I sway back and forth, gazing down at it.

"Because it was made for you," he mumbles.

Before I question him further, he grips my elbow and ushers me toward the door. Deciding it's not worth it, I pad after him. We've just stepped over the threshold when he stutters to a stop and holds up his hand.

I wait while he dashes back inside and pulls on his own clothes. I smother a giggle. He shakes his head before grabbing something else from the trunk, then returns with shoes. Thankfully, they're flats, but the actual name escapes me. He drops to one knee and slips them on.

"If you want to explore, so be it. However, we will be doing this my way. If you do not obey—"

"I know, I know. Punishment." I snort as we descend the stairs. "You realize if you actually want to punish me, handing out orgasms like they're candy might not be the best way to do it."

I bite my lip, wishing I would have kept my mouth shut. While I'm not complaining about his methods, I don't want him to stop. If he thinks they're ineffectual, he might deny me outright.

I glance at him, almost missing a step. He rights me before I can tumble the rest of the way down the stairs. He stops on the landing and crowds me against the wall. My breath stalls in my chest as his cock, already hard again, presses into my stomach.

He levels me with a piercing stare. "This is serious, Melody. The tunnels within these walls can be deadly. I will not risk your life for a moment of pleasure. Tell me now if you're not capable of following directions."

"I'll listen. But you'll be there if anything goes wrong, so I don't see how I could fuck that up." My stomach flips, both from his nearness and the thought of falling down the stairs and breaking my neck.

He grins, but it's not the carefree one from before. There's an edge to it that sends flames licking through me. His tongue darts out and he licks his bottom lip, pulling my eyes down. I never noticed how plump they are, though I've experienced the pleasure they force from my body.

Even now, when he's barely even touching me, I'm on the brink of doing something very out of character for me. Biting him right now probably wouldn't be the best idea since he's trying to be serious.

"I won't be there to save you, only catch you. And when I do, I'll remind you who you belong to."

I suck in a shuddering breath. "What do I do?"

"Follow the music. If you lose the melody, start again. If I catch you before you reach the end..." His eyes turn dark, lust dripping from his gaze. He reaches behind me and pushes on the wall. A panel pops open, swinging inward to reveal a dark passageway.

"One last thing, little muse," he says, and I glance back at him. "Run."

It takes a second to process his command. Once I do, my eyes widen, and I scramble into the black void. I don't know what the hell he was talking about, but I've found I rarely understand the words coming out of his mouth. He's an enigma I desperately want to solve.

I stumble a few feet in before I hit a wall. If I didn't have my hands in front of me, I would have smashed my face into it. I've dealt with enough blood tonight. Actually, I didn't deal with Chad at all. Xavier did all the work.

As I shuffle through the dark space, twists and turns appearing out of nowhere, I realize most of what's happened tonight has been guided by Xavier. I haven't made any decisions. And I didn't care. I just went along with all of it. There's something freeing about that I didn't anticipate.

"Remember the music," Xavier calls, his voice nowhere and everywhere all at the same time.

I pull in a calming breath, keeping my hand on one wall as I continue onward. If I didn't know any better, I'd say he threw me into a pitch-black room and is merely watching me go around in circles.

And then I hit the first staircase. I miss the first step, then skip down three more before I stop my downward spiral. Metal rings out and the cold railing curves under my fingers.

Glancing behind me, my heartbeat thunders in my ears. No distant lights. No muffled footsteps. Just silence wrapped in darkness.

"Follow the music," I mutter, blinking rapidly.

I start humming as I slowly pad down the rest of the stairs. It's not until I reach the bottom that I realize I'm singing the piece Xavier was writing. The one he played for me while I fucked him. The one that rings in my ears every time he's inside me. The one he says he wrote for us.

Somehow, after only a few times hearing it, my mind picked up on the notes—the harmony and melody weaving together seamlessly. I may play the xylophone well, but I've never been the best at picking up songs quickly. I certainly cannot play by ear like others can.

Reading the sheet music and practicing it over and over until it's woven into my muscle memory is how I was able to rise in the ranks within orchestras. Others relied on their natural talent. I just busted my ass.

I continue to hum as words form in my mind. Symphonies don't typically have lyrics, but they dance in my head anyway. Perhaps he was writing an opera and our song was merely the beginning of it. I imagine he had his hand in quite a few of those when he opened this place.

Another turn comes out of nowhere and I lose what little grasp I had on the song. I stop, closing my eyes and pulling in another deep breath to calm my nerves. I was so distracted thinking about the music and the history of the theatre, I forgot what I was doing. I begin again slowly, then yelp as a steady thud echoes through the air. It sounds like a mallet hitting wood. My skin prickles and I spin around.

Dashing forward, I capture the music once more, humming louder than before. A flash of white next to me has me skittering to a stop. It's faded by the time I fully turned. The thumping increases, along with the low strain of our song. The white spot pulses as I join in, and a musical staff appears, the swirling lines of a treble clef ending in a flourish.

Follow the music.

Of course he would have some random magical way to lead me wherever he wants me to go. A giddiness floods me and I hurry for the next glowing symbol farther along, singing the entire way.

As I near the next treble clef, Xavier's voice dims and I cackle in anticipation. Gradually, they become a trail marching off into the dark and I gather up my skirts. Running in the dark with nothing more than some strange glowing signs to guide me could land me in a world of trouble, but Xavier hasn't led me astray yet.

It's not until I reach a space lined with mirrors that I start second-guessing that decision. Spinning around, I try to find the real treble clef that will lead me out of here, but it's not as if the actual one is any different from the reflections.

I press my fingers against the cool surface, my pale face staring back at me. The thrumming of the mallet against wood ceases, sending my heart racing again.

I hum faster, though this time it's "I'm a Little Teapot." Everything glows brighter, lighting up the room. Frantically, I move from one to another. None of them give.

A choked sob leaves me while my chest thrums in anticipation. The mix of emotions has my voice wavering, yet I keep singing. If what little light I have leaves, I won't be able to cope. All the excitement of Xavier chasing me will bleed away, leaving only terror.

The room is circular, seemingly enclosed with no way out. My breath saws in and out of my chest as I reach the mirror I'm pretty sure I started with.

Stomping my foot, I let out a small scream of frustration.

Xavier obviously knows where I am, so it doesn't matter. I wasn't trying to hide from him, anyway. In fact, right now him finding me might be the only way I'll get out of this maze.

Resting my forehead against the glass, I let the cold seep into my skin. The soft glow begins to dim, and I push back. Just as the darkness bleeds into the space, I pull in a deep breath and sing.

It's an old song. One my grandmother used to hum in the kitchen. She claimed it helped me fall asleep, but I remember all the words. The symbols blaze to life around me and I close my eyes. As the last notes fade, I peek at the mirror, hoping something else will appear other than my own reflection.

I gasp as a shadow detaches from behind me and Xavier steps into view. His dark eyes bore into me. The hair on the back of my neck rises as he slips closer.

An exhilarating thrill unfurls inside of me. I should run away, put some distance between us. Giving myself over to him for whatever punishment he has in store doesn't sound like such a bad idea, though. I glance around subtly, waiting for a hole to open up so I can dash through.

There's nowhere to run. I'm well and truly caught.

Chapter Sixteen

Xavier

Relief floods my system, threatening to overwhelm me. I was worried Melody wouldn't be able to handle something like this. I should have known better. She was made for me, delivered by whatever wretched curse caught me in its web. Perhaps fate now feels guilty for putting such a burden on me. I won't complain. Melody is everything I've ever dreamed of.

Whether or not she knew her singing would lead me straight to her makes little difference. From the gleam in her eyes, she wanted me to find her—to claim her. While my instinct would be to punish her for allowing herself to be caught, I don't have it in me. Taking her will be enough. If she tries to run again, all the better.

Her breath hitches as I slide my fingers into her hair. Wrapping the strands around my hand, I grip her locks and force her face toward the mirror. Her palms slap against the glass, and her eyes meet mine in the reflection as her breath fogs the surface, obscuring her image.

I lean close, pressing my chest to her back and whisper in her ear, "Caught you."

Her body trembles and her forehead thumps next to her hands. I force her head back, relishing her compliance. I wouldn't be surprised if she wants this more than I do. When I brush my lips across her skin, a needy sound escapes her and my cock twitches.

"You wanted to be caught, didn't you?"

"Yes," she breathes.

I hum, wanting more from her. I want everything she has, everything she is. Nothing would be greater than if she gave herself entirely over to me.

As she sways in my arms, I realize she already has. She's utterly enchanting, completely at my mercy. The trust she's handing to me is a precious thing I won't take for granted.

My hand slides down her stomach until I cup her cunt, and she gasps, eyes flying open. Even through the layers of fabric, the heat emanating from her is intoxicating. Her mouth parts, small whimpers leaving her as I flex my hand still gripping her hair.

"Open your eyes," I command. They flutter open and find mine in the reflection. "Such a beauty. Be a good girl and keep your gaze fixed on your body as I give you exactly what you want—what you need."

"Yes, maestro." Her lips twitch, and a rumble rolls through my chest.

"Careful, little vixen. Mocking will lead to more punishment. And I have more than withholding orgasms in store for you if you continue."

Her face lights up, a bright flame dancing in her eyes. "Care to share?"

I growl and release her body. Her hands twitch as if she'll drop them, and I grip her neck. She presses her lips together, and I drop my hand to my pants. The more time we spend together, the bolder she gets. I can't say it's an unwelcome turn of events. I pull my cock out and her eyes widen. When her tongue darts out, I glance away.

Scrubbing a hand down my face, I attempt to get myself under control. It's hard enough having her like this. If I lose all sense, I'll end up hurting her. The thought only sends a flurry of images behind my lids. Her ass in the air with my handprint gracing her skin. My marks littered across her flesh. Melody tied to my bed, blindfolded and at my mercy. Chasing her should have been enough to rein in the insatiable beast inside me. Apparently not.

I quiver when her hot breath ghosts across my cock. I was so absorbed as I fantasized of the many ways I could take her, I didn't hear her moving. She gazes up at me from her knees. When her mouth opens, I suck in a sharp breath. Her tongue darts out again, this time to lick the drop gathered at the tip. I shudder and my length twitches. Her lips close over my cock, and I groan, unable to hold back the primal sound any longer.

My hand dives into her hair, wrapping around the strands once more. Her nails dig into my thighs as I attempt to hold still and allow her to explore. If she keeps up the seductive noises she's making, I'll end up fucking her mouth without regard. I wonder if that's exactly what she wants.

With one hand still gripping her hair, I bring the other to her cheek. Her eyes meet mine and I force her to take more of my length. She coughs, then swallows, and I grit my teeth.

"You're so beautiful with my cock in your mouth. Do you want me to come down your throat, little muse?"

Her eyes twinkle and I swear she smiles. The urge to thrust into her hard overtakes me and she chokes, tears springing to her eyes as I hit the back of her throat.

Easing back, I stroke her cheek. Her nostrils flare and I bury my cock into her again—over and over until my stomach tightens. Every muscle in my body seizes as I bottom out one last time, holding her head while she gags. She swallows every drop like the good girl she is.

As I pull back, her teeth graze the underside of my shaft and I growl her name. The innocent look she plasters on her face doesn't fool me. I force her upright and spin her around. Crowding her against the mirror, I press my body into hers. My cock hardens again, regardless of the fact I just came. It's one of the few benefits of the curse. I'm sure it was meant as a punish-ment—always hard but never fully sated. Tonight, I couldn't be happier for such a blessing. Being able to fuck her again and again, bringing her pleasure multiple times, is a gift I'll thank the wretched spirit for.

"Seems to me you want to be a brat," I murmur in her ear, and she shudders. "That's what they call women who do such things these days, yes?"

"I don't know what you're talking about." She gasps as I snake my hand under her dress and knead the flesh of her ass.

"Are you sure?" I slide my hand to her pussy and groan. "Even with your behavior, you're soaking wet. I didn't realize having my cock in your mouth would have this effect."

"Bold of you to assume it has anything to do with you," she wheezes as I slide my finger through her folds.

I growl, sliding my other hand from the back of her neck to her throat. She whimpers and her eyes fall closed as a flush splashes across her cheeks. A low whine leaves her when I pull my fingers from between her legs. Gripping my length, I line myself up with her core. Her mouth opens, probably to wield a sarcastic diatribe.

I thrust hard and her pussy clenches, holding my cock deep inside her. A strangled noise leaves me as she spasms around me in time with my heartbeat.

She laughs breathlessly, and I realize she's doing it on purpose. Seizing control again, I flex my fingers around her throat, gripping her hip with the other.

I slam into her harder and faster than before. I should slow, put her pleasure at the forefront of my mind. My baser instincts take over, the need for control riding me.

Every time I bottom out, a grunt bursts from me. I dip my head and sink my teeth into her neck. Her desperate cries echo around us, mingling with the low strains of music flowing through the stagnant air.

"Xavier," she moans, my name on her lips more of a plea than anything else.

I freeze, our bodies molded together. Clenching my jaw, I roll my hips, earning another whimper from her. The emotions building inside me are more than I can handle.

I may love being lost in her cunt, but the feelings she pulls from me are something I've never experienced before. If fate was kind, I'd never be parted from her, spending my days worshiping her body, building a life with her, loving her. She'd never want for anything if I had a say.

"Something you needed, sweet Melody?" I force the words out as fire licks at my throat.

"Don't stop. Don't you dare fucking stop."

I roll my hips again and she shudders. "Give yourself to me—wholly and completely and I'll let you come."

"I don't know what that means," she whines as she pushes back, trying to force me deeper. I doubt that's possible. I don't know where I end and she begins. As it should be.

I pull out of her slowly until only the tip remains, then plunge into her again. The bond between us flares to life, linking us together. No matter what happens after tonight, nothing will sever the connection. Forever, she'll be mine. Her body tenses, then relaxes, a weightlessness overtaking her. I hold her up with an arm around her waist and my chest against her back.

"You're mine," I growl, burying my cock into her.

"Yours," she pants.

As soon as her confession leaves her lips, I surge into her, owning her mind, body, and soul. Her cunt quivers as she nears the edge of oblivion. I hiss and pull from her heat. A sob leaves her, but I don't plan on punishing her anymore. I spin her around and grip her ass before picking her up, then slam her against the mirror.

I plunge into her again and her legs wrap around my waist. She grips my shoulders, nails digging through the fabric of my shirt. She thrashes in my arms as I fuck her.

Within seconds, she jerks, head knocking against the glass as she comes apart. I don't slow, though I memorize the look on her face as she orgasms. My heartbeat is a metronome, keeping time as she pulses around my cock.

"One more. Show me how much your pussy loves me fucking you."

"I can't," she sobs, clinging to me.

"You can. And you will," I snarl. "Touch yourself as I take this sweet little cunt."

She shudders, hooded eyes finding mine. Her hand drops between her legs and her knuckles brush my length as I slam into her, never slowing. I hold my own release at bay, keeping my gaze fixed on hers. If I watch her playing with her clit, I'll explode. And I refuse to come before she does once more.

I thought my control would come from overpowering her. In fact, her submission fractures whatever dominance I sought. I no longer need it. I merely need to watch her fall apart in my arms and my composure crumbles.

Music erupts around us as she shatters, body convulsing as she climaxes. I glance down, mesmerized by my cock disappearing into her cunt. The sight is too much, and I follow her into oblivion. I slam my mouth on hers, groaning as I empty inside of her.

She winds her arms around my neck, kissing me with a fervor I've never experienced. Our tongues tangle together as we float in the blissfulness of being one.

I pull back, slipping out of her, and her feet hit the floor. I drop to my knees and shove her dress up. The evidence of our exploits once again seep out of her and my mouth waters.

I wrap my hand around the back of her thigh, keeping her still as I swipe my fingers through the mess we've made. She shudders, body curling over mine as she clings to me to stay upright.

My thumb circles her clit as I push my fingers inside her. Her delicious cunt spasms and I grin. She gathers the hem of her dress and peers down at me with wide eyes.

"I can't. I just—" She sucks in a sharp breath and her gaze fixes on me as I stroke her.

"You can. And you will. This body belongs to me. This exquisite little cunt belongs to me. Your pleasure belongs to me. If I tell you to come again, you will."

Her hand clutches her dress and her mouth parts, desire flaming to life in her eyes. I curl my fingers, dragging them out of her before plunging back in. With each thrust, she trembles and her cunt quivers. As I rub her clit, satisfaction flows through me, knowing I can bring her such ecstasy.

Her body tenses and she surrenders to the pleasure. It's a quiet rapture instead of the intenseness from before. She hums, a soft smile gracing her lips.

Gently, I pull my hand from between her legs and stand. Wrapping her in my arms, I hold her while she trembles. When she tips her head back, I hold my still glistening fingers to her mouth.

She opens without a word, and I slide them in. Her tongue swirls around them, licking them clean. A surge of longing hits me, and once again I'm hard. As much as I'd love to sink into her heat again, she needs rest. I may not be able to give her much, but a slight reprieve costs me nothing.

As I gaze at her, I mourn the fact I can't give her more. That I can't give her everything.

Chapter Seventeen

Melody

"Why didn't the symbols disappear?" I ask as I fluff my dress.

I refuse to look him in the eye, too embarrassed by the fact that I just begged this man to fuck me. I've never been so needy before. He didn't seem to mind. Actually, he seems to prefer me several different ways. I slough off the feelings and throw back my shoulders. When I glance at him, he's smirking. Again.

"Something funny?" I demand, planting my hands on my hips.

He tilts his head. "Would you care to discuss that little transformation you just went through?"

"No. I'd rather not." I shake my head, sniffing as I glance around.

His hand wraps around my throat, and I gasp. He forces my back to the mirror, and I shiver when his thumb caresses my jaw, then swipes across my lips.

He leans in close and whispers in my ear, "Tell me. Divulge your darkest secrets, my sweet little muse."

His voice, laced with seduction, makes my knees weak. There's a flutter in my stomach. I felt it every time I stepped foot in this place. I felt it every time I played the xylophone. I felt it when we first met and every time his eyes find mine.

I thought it was his charisma. Why else would he be able to convince me to fuck him all over this damn theatre? Now I recognize it for what it truly is—the mysterious connection he talked about.

"You bring out a side of me I should be embarrassed by. Instead..." I let my words trail off, glancing away from him.

He forces my gaze back to him as his fingers dig into my skin. "Instead?"

"I crave you." The words fall from me unbidden.

I expect his familiar smirk to bloom across his face, but instead there's a softness in his eyes that wasn't there before. And the ever-present hunger I'm starting to suspect is just for me.

He won't laugh because he feels it too—the ache for more. Of him. Of his body. For all that he is to possess every inch of me. It's why I didn't complain when he sunk his teeth into my flesh, marking me clear as day for anyone to see. It's why I didn't question the dirty words he murmured into my skin.

His lips brush against mine, then he steps back. An empty pit opens in my chest, threatening to suck me into its nothingness. He must see the devastation in my eyes since he pulls my body into his.

"I'll show you the lake beneath our feet. I'll even fuck you next to the water's edge, if you so please." He nips at my bottom lip. "Then we'll watch the sunrise from the bell tower. With the whole of the city laid out before us, I'll make you scream my name into the heavens."

Without warning, he grabs my hand and tugs me toward a mirror. The reflection of the treble clef wavers and I yank my hand away. Xavier scowls over his shoulder and snatches my elbow. I scream as he shoves me into the mirror.

Stumbling, I throw my hands in front of me. Instead of a solid surface, I'm met with a black void of nothingness. Except there's wood beneath my feet and a wall at my back.

My head whips back and forth, searching for any bit of light. Xavier's warmth seeps into me as he steps through the mirror. I whirl around, and he grabs my hips to keep us from falling. My hands land on his chest, and my heart skips a beat.

More symbols blaze to life around us, some floating in the air while others march off into the darkness. He spins me in his arms, and I lean against him.

"There's no music," I murmur. I've almost become used to the layers of sound dancing around us. Now it's just silence.

"We are the music, Melody. It lives within us, therefore they appear to light our way. Come." He steps around me and grabs my hand once more.

I sigh, still not fully understanding. Music has always lived within me. It's filled my soul in a way nothing else has. No one understood the attachment I had to it.

When my parents paid attention, they mocked my dreams of playing in an orchestra. My classmates avoided me since it was all I talked about. Eventually, I stopped trying to explain the visceral need to play. I thought I'd meet other musicians and they'd understand, but it never happened. Xavier, though...the music calls to him as well.

"Pay attention or you'll fall." Xavier's voice jars me from my thoughts. "I may not be harmed should I plummet over the edge, but I fear you would."

I glance around, realizing we're halfway across a small walk-way. The railing only comes up to my waist. The glowing light doesn't reach very far, and I shiver, pressing closer to Xavier's back.

He chuckles and squeezes my hand. I'm sure he means it to be comforting, but it doesn't work. I'm practically tripping over his heels by the time we reach the other side.

We crouch, slipping through a small doorway. When I stand up, my head thuds into the ceiling. I duck again and rub my head. He sighs but doesn't say anything.

I'm about to lose my shit if he doesn't hurry. There isn't

enough room in this small space. Just when I'm about to freak the fuck out, the hallway widens, and I suck in a deep breath. I'm pretty sure I was holding it without noticing.

"Do they use the walkway during the plays?" If I ask enough questions, maybe I'll be able to ignore the other things that seem to be determined to scare the shit out of me.

"Not publicly. No one knows of these hidden passageways anymore. I suspect that's a good thing. We lost many people within this secret place."

"What the hell does that mean?" Something brushes my arm and I screech, ripping my hand from his. Another light touch at the back of my neck and I yelp as I bat it away.

Xavier hauls my back to his chest, trapping my arms against my sides. Tears spring to my eyes and a shrill noise leaves me. He shushes me, curling his body around mine.

"It's just a curtain, Melody. Nothing more. This space is designed to play tricks on your mind, but it's merely an illusion." He turns me and I bury my face into his chest. "Did you think I wouldn't keep you safe?"

"I don't know if I like this. I need a flashlight. Shit, I don't even have my phone. I left it in your room." I'm babbling. I can't help it.

He pulls me after him again. "I'm not familiar with a flashlight. The symbols and my memory are enough to guide me. I assume a phone was the device in your hands earlier. I don't know how that would help us, though I suppose it did light up in a way."

My mouth drops open as I stumble along. The longer he talks, the more he reveals. Either he is a very good actor, dedicated to the part he's playing, or he truly is a man trapped in a theatre. My mind skips back to every interaction we've had. All of it reinforces the idea. This, more than anything else, convinces me. A peace settles over me and I accept my fate.

I could stay here. With him. I could spend my days practicing and my nights learning the secrets of the theatre with him. A choked sob leaves me, and I smother it behind my hand when I realize my fairy tale imaginings are unrealistic.

Nothing ties me to the outside world. But if Xavier really does disappear into the xylophone for most of the time, I'd be alone here. I don't know if it would be any different from living in my apartment, but sleeping in his bed by myself might feel awkward. Then again, his bed is exceptionally comfortable.

"What are you pondering back there?" he asks, breaking into my thoughts once more.

"How do you break the curse?" The second the words are spoken, I regret them.

He tenses, fingers flexing around mine. "I'm unsure. That was never explained to me."

"What was explained to you? How did it happen? What did it feel like?"

He sighs, shaking his head as we step into another room—a landing, actually. Stairs march down into the darkness, the symbols winking out of existence. I peer over my shoulder, counting the seconds as the way we came plunges into darkness.

"Perhaps we should find another subject to explore."

"But if we could reverse it..."

He crowds me against the wall, his body pressing into mine. "You cannot save me from my fate, Melody. You're better off running far from me and what I am."

Silence descends on us like a heavy blanket over my senses. His chest heaves, his harsh breath sawing in and out of him. Whatever happened to him, he clearly hasn't dealt with it.

I can't imagine being trapped somewhere, much less my entire existence snuffed out with no warning. Gently, I lift my hand and cup his cheek. He presses his face into my palm. I close my eyes, silently lending whatever strength I can.

"What do you think you are?"

He huffs, pushing away from me. "Someone who does not deserve your pity, nor your sympathy. A monster. Now and always, I am a creature cursed to spend what little time I have as a human in the darkest of nights. I shouldn't have taken you—claimed you. You were too intoxicating. You drew me in, weaving your magic around me. And now, I fear I won't be able to let you go when the sun rises."

"Maybe I don't want to be released. Did it ever occur to you I might actually *want* to stay? Maybe I feel the connection between us, too. Maybe I know there's something else at work here and I found exactly where I belong. Did you ever think of that?"

"You don't mean that," he snarls, pacing away, and his form vanishes.

I creep forward, trying to find him in the dark. I really don't want to slip down the stairs and break my neck. That wouldn't help either of us. After an agonizing amount of time, my knuckles sweep across fabric. I flatten my palm against his shoulder, and he shudders.

I didn't realize I had such an effect on him. Every time he touches me, hell, every time he's within ten feet of me, I'm drawn to him. I smile at the thought of not being alone with the feeling. I wrap my arms around his waist and rest my cheek on his back. His fingers tangle with mine, holding me to him.

Hours. That's all the time we've had together, yet it feels like we've spent a lifetime together. And still, it's not enough.

"I want to see the lake. And the bell tower. If you abandon me now, I'll get lost down here, and I'm going to be honest, I might freak out then. I don't do well with dark places." I don't know anyone who would feel comfortable down here other than him. Given the opportunity, I could get used to it, though. If only he'll give me a chance.

"I would never abandon you, Melody," he mutters harshly, as if I've offended him. "We're almost there."

He tugs me down the stairs. Ones I clearly can't see. The light has abandoned us. If the music lives in us, it's clearly because of Xavier's sudden shift in attitude.

I wonder if he'll get over it by the time we get there. I was looking forward to him taking me on the edge of a lake. Getting sand up my ass doesn't sound great, though. I snort and his feet scuffle against the ground, then stop.

I slam into his back, and he grunts. Rolling my eyes, I step back. It's not like I bowled him over. He's a brick wall, muscles layered upon muscles.

"Is this how you've always looked, or do you work out?" I realize I'm babbling and saying whatever asinine thing pops into my head. If he'd stop spouting about being a monster and get back to fucking me, I wouldn't feel the need.

I take another step back, wondering when I became a sex-crazed fool. Going so long without indulging in afternoon delights seems to have messed with my brain.

I snort, knowing it's just him. That's the conclusion I've come to every time I question myself or him or either of our motives. It's just who he is. It's some strange magic or curse. Something in the beyond driving this wild night.

"Are you going to be like this the rest of the night?" I whine, tugging away from him and crossing my arms. "Because I, for one, do not enjoy this part."

A torch flares to life next to me and I yelp, skipping away from it. The fire cast deep shadows across half his face, accentuating his sharp jaw.

He grabs the torch and gestures behind him. "There's a boat just beyond the light. It will take you to the outside. Unless you jump over the side, that is."

"Are you breaking up with me?" I slap my hand over my mouth, horror dousing me.

He shakes his head, unable to look me in the eye. We're not dating. He probably doesn't even understand what I'm talking about. In one night, I feel like I've gained and lost him. Calling me his doesn't mean anything in the heat of the moment. I should have remembered that. And now I'm stuck with a heartbreak that shouldn't be this devastating.

Yet my world is crumbling around me, and there's nothing I can do about it.

Chapter Eighteen

Xavier

I don't fully understand the alarm in Melody's eyes. Our time together was always fleeting. Never enough. We have no future. Her being here should end now.

As much as I selfishly want to keep her here, experience what little time we have left together, it's not fair to her. Keeping her here with me...it does neither of us any good.

She needs to leave before I do something I'll regret—like lock her in my attic with the hope I'll return after the next performance. Being trapped in the xylophone without her would be torturous. If I let her go, she can live her life free of the constraints my existence would place on her.

"We have, at most, an hour before the sun rises. I'd rather you not be here when that happens," I say gruffly.

I gesture toward the boat again, and she steps away from me —away from the lake. Tipping my head back, I suck in a calming breath. I won't force her. I sure as hell won't abandon her. But her staying isn't an option.

All my plans to fuck her next to the lake, to show her the bell tower, crumbled under the weight of reality. I am a monster who should never have claimed her. Decades later and I'm still making the same mistakes I did all those years ago.

"You're an asshole," she seethes, and I blink at her impassively.

Her hands curl into fists by her sides, and I wonder if she'll hit me. I wouldn't stop her. I deserve her wrath. Tipping my chin, I acknowledge the truth of her statement, which only seems to piss her off more.

"What about all those things you said? The promises you made?"

"I made no promises, Melody. There is nothing I can give you other than your freedom. I suggest you take it."

"Or what?"

She crosses her arms over her chest, causing her breasts to practically spill from the neckline of her dress. My eyes dip down, then shoot back to her face. She smirks and her gaze fixates on my cock straining against my pants.

"Your decisions are your own, as they have always been."

She scoffs, glancing away, and I swear there's a sheen to her eyes. "You're a coward. That's why you were cursed. You ran when others needed you. And you didn't learn your lesson one bit. Instead of fighting for us—to see if there's something actually here—you're pushing me away. Because you're afraid of what?"

I explode, throwing the torch to the ground and snarling as I seize her arms. She gasps, but there's no fear in her eyes. I grind my teeth together, resisting the urge to shake her. She doesn't understand what I'm trying to save her from. She's right. I was a fucking coward, but letting her go isn't something I would have done before.

"I'm afraid for you," I growl. "Nothing good can come from you staying here any longer."

Her face softens as our eyes meet. She reaches up, cupping my cheek. Her gentle touch is my undoing. Whatever arguments I had vanish in the wake of her caresses.

Her thumb grazes my bottom lip, and I nip at it. Skimming my palms down her arms, I settle them on her hips and tug her closer. As her body aligns with mine, the ache in my chest eases.

"You promised me a night. I expect you to honor that," she whispers.

Her hand slips to the back of my neck, and she drags my head down. I groan before covering her mouth with my own. Even knowing I should let go, I can't. My defenses have well and truly disappeared with her. I should have known Melody wouldn't give in so easily and it would test my own resolve. In the back of my mind, I knew I would surrender to her given the chance.

Digging my fingers into her ass, I massage her flesh as I devour her. She gasps, ripping her mouth from mine and arching her back. I take full advantage, scraping my teeth against the sensitive skin of her neck. When she moans, the last of my resolve winks out, leaving desire to fill the voids left behind.

I pick her up, molding her body to mine, and her legs wrap around me. I sink my teeth into her heaving breast and her fingers latch onto my hair, tugging roughly at the strands. There aren't many places to fuck her properly here. It won't stop me from plunging into her heat once more. My cock throbs as she rubs against me.

"Fuck me, Xavier. Now." The command in her tone strikes a chord within me. It resonates through the air, creating a whole new song I've never heard before.

I stalk to the edge of the water and drop my hold on her. She yelps, scrambling to set her feet on the soft sand. I cup her breasts through her dress, playing with her nipples before grasping the neckline.

Her eyes flutter closed and I smirk, then rip the fabric from her body. Her moan catches me off guard. Dipping my head, I lick my lips, then latch onto one of the hard nubs I've exposed.

She squirms, attempting to free her arms. I release her nipple and wrap my arms around her. The fabric at her neck splits, leaving the dress in tatters. At one time, I would have cared. Now, the material is merely a hindrance standing in my way of worshiping her body. Her sleeves shimmy off her hands and the rest of the fabric gathers at her hips.

Pulling back, I survey her from the flush on her cheeks to her bare toes curling into the sand. She lost her shoes somewhere along the way. I grab her wrist, yanking her into me once more. Her fingers grasp at the hem of my shirt, trying to remove it completely.

I chuckle at her attempts before I take pity on her and whip it over my head. She's already moved onto my pants. By the time my shirt flutters to the ground, she has the button undone. My cock springs free as she tugs the zipper down and licks her lips.

Seizing her chin, I raise an eyebrow. "On your hands and knees, little muse."

She huffs as I drop my hold on her. Her bottom lip pops out as she pouts. "Please?"

I snort, glancing over my shoulder at the lake. I'd rather not be down here when the sun rises. If she takes my cock in her mouth again, we might never make it to the bell tower.

A grunt escapes me when her tongue darts out, licking my tip. She's taken the decision away from me and dropped to her knees. Her small hand wraps around the base and a primal noise leaves me.

Before I can protest at the lack of time, her mouth closes around my cock. My fingers slide into her hair, and I hold her in place while I thrust to the back of her throat. She gags, then hums her pleasure. Her hand drops between her legs, and I pull from her mouth while she protests.

"Was I not clear? I told you, hands and knees. If you're so eager to please me, then suck my cock. But you won't touch yourself. Understood?" I wait until she nods before I slide the tip between her lips again. "Don't forget to breathe."

I thrust into her mouth and tears spring to her eyes. Her head bobs, taking as much of me as she can, never once complaining. Never once hesitating. As much as I'm convinced I'm no good for her, she's meant for me. She's mine. The connection between us is a living, breathing thing, but I never fully understood it.

Until now.

As my muscles tense and my cock swells, Melody swallows, her throat squeezing me. My orgasm catches me by surprise, and I lurch forward. She coughs and I pull from her mouth.

I drop to my knees in front of her, swiping my thumb across her lips. Her tongue darts out, licking the wetness from the pad, and I push it into her mouth. Her eyes fall closed as she shudders.

"Such a wanton creature you are," I murmur as I pull my thumb from her mouth.

I stand, tapping her head to keep her in place as I prowl to her side. She glances over her shoulder and raises a single brow, but the ravenous need in her eyes gives her away.

Her body trembles when I guide her onto her hands and knees. I slide off my pants and kick them aside before settling behind her. I gather her skirts and flip them to the side. The cold of the sand seeps into my skin, and I grip her hip with one hand. With the other, I explore her flesh, then slip my fingers between her legs.

Her sweet nectar coats my palm as I press my hand against her cunt. When my thumb flicks her clit, she groans, arching her back. She pushes her ass into me, trying to force my fingers into her core, and my cock hardens again. Her body always demands more. Yet it's never enough. I'd never tire of her, no matter how many centuries we might have been granted in another life.

"Stop teasing me," she sobs as she rocks back and forth.

I continue to stroke her, staying away from her core and sliding her clit between my fingers. "What do you need, little muse?"

"I need you inside me. I can't—" Her words dissolve into a whimper and her head drops.

"I should make you suffer some more," I say thoughtfully.

With my fingers still stroking her, I reach around and pinch her nipple, then roll it into a tight nub. She bucks against me, a shallow sob leaving her as I move to her other breast. Sitting back, I skim my hand across her ass, admiring the luscious canvas in front of me.

"Bastard," she gasps, and I smirk.

I swat her, then flatten my palm to her skin. Her yelp echoes through the space and I caress the print I've left behind. The urge to do it again engulfs me. My cock twitches and I spank her again. Wetness gushes from her cunt, covering my fingers that are still stroking her.

"Would you like to continue to call me names?" I ask through gritted teeth, attempting to hold my desire to plunge into her heat.

If we had the time, I'd paint her flesh with the same crimson flush that's spreading across her beautiful ass. She pants as she sways, her breasts creating a tantalizing pendulum. What I wouldn't give to worship them for the rest of the night. An ache settles in my chest, dangerously close to my heart.

"If you'd make me come, we wouldn't *be* in this position," she snarls, then pushes back into my hand.

I smack her again, the loud crack echoing around us, and she cries out, her tone laced with pleasure—a need from deep within her desperate for release. My thumb finds her clit and I circle it. Her cunt clenches around my fingers and her back arches.

"Oh f-fuck," she stutters out. "What the—don't. No."

I chuckle as my hand drops away from between her legs. She slaps the ground, though the sand muffles any irritation she's attempting to convey. She does it again for good measure, then glares at me over her shoulder.

"Something amiss, Melody?" I ask before popping my fingers in my mouth. I'll never tire of the taste of her on my tongue.

Her mouth drops open, then snaps shut as she resumes her glaring. I lick the evidence of her orgasm from my skin. Whatever she was going to snap at me is lost. Not that I would have heard her. I'm too busy enjoying the fruits of my labor.

"I think I prefer when you're spouting about the music in the air instead of—" She waves her hand in my direction. "Whatever this is. Arrogant asshole."

"Oh, you prefer me both ways, Melody. You cannot fool me.

Now, are you going to be a good girl and take my cock? Or are we going to have to explore other punishments that drive you wild?" I raise an eyebrow and tilt my head.

She scoffs, rolling her eyes. "I doubt you..."

I skim my fingers across her flesh, still red from my palm. "You were saying?"

A dangerous glint enters her eyes, and I pause.

"I can be your good girl."

Chapter Nineteen

Melody

I drop my head again, unable to keep the smirk from my lips. The shock on Xavier's face is almost too much. My shoulders shake no matter how I try to keep my laughter in.

His hand comes down on my ass again and I whimper, all the humor gone. My pussy clenches around nothing, leaving me empty and throbbing. As much as I'm enjoying this particular punishment, I'd like it more if he'd fill me up the way I'm craving.

I'm surprised I'm still aching for him. I've lost count of how many orgasms I've had. It feels cliché to fall back on the connection we have, but there's no other plausible explanation.

With my lackluster experience, I never expected I'd be in this position. And I refuse to complain about it. My body craves more —more of him, more of everything he gives me.

"Is that so?" he murmurs.

I shake my head, and a chill rolls up my back. "I told you what you wanted to hear."

His teeth sink into my ass, right where he swatted me. I swallow the moan begging to escape. When he releases my flesh, his hand rubs the spot. If he was anyone else, I'd have kicked him in the face. With Xavier, I'm slightly terrified I'd let him do whatever he wants to my body and love every fucking minute of it.

"And therein lies the issue. Telling me what I want to hear isn't the same. You don't *want* to be my good girl. You want to be punished, don't you?" The low rumble of his voice reverberates through my body, sending another bolt of lust straight to my pussy.

"I want whatever is going to get you to fuck me," I snarl, glaring at him.

His body covers mine, his strong arm wrapping around my waist while his fingers pinch my nipple. His cock slides between my legs, but not where I want him most. I grunt, exasperation making my movements erratic, and I almost crash onto my face. Of course, he catches me, his hand slamming into the sand next to mine.

"Keep that up and we won't make it to the bell tower," he murmurs in my ear, then nips at the lobe.

"If *you* keep it up, I won't get to come again."

He *tsks*, his hand exploring my body as he rubs his cock against my wetness. Every time he hits my clit, I let loose another gasp. Even knowing he's teasing me, I can't keep my comments to myself. It's as if someone else, perhaps the wanton creature he accused me of being, has taken over my body.

"Never fear, little muse. Haven't I proven I'll give you exactly what you need?"

I open my mouth to snap back at him, but a hiss leaves me instead as he rolls my nipple between his fingers again. Suddenly, he sits back and his hands grip the skirts pooled around my waist. If I hadn't been so far gone in my pleasure, I would have mourned the loss of the dress. I close my eyes, waiting for him to make his move. The fabric digs into my hips, and I focus on it rather than the pulsing ache working its way through my body.

"Fuck me or I'll take care of it myself," I growl.

He plunges his cock into me and I groan, dropping onto my elbows. His shirt appears under my face seconds before he wraps his hand in my hair and forces my head down. As soon as I'm splayed before him, ass in the air, he pulls out and slams into me again. He fucks me hard and fast—a punishment all on its own.

Within seconds I spasm, crying out as waves of pleasurable relief wash over me. He keeps up his frantic pace, merely grunting as I clench around his length. The ringing in my ears amplifies, and I close my eyes. When the noise recedes, the air fills with a familiar tune. Xavier hums as he slows, then rolls his hips.

"Such a beautiful sight," he mutters, digging his fingers into my waist. "What I wouldn't give to take you like this again and again. To tie you to my bed and fuck you until you were hoarse from screaming my name. To lay you out on the stage again and put on our own personal opera."

He continues whispering his fantasies of all the ways he'd dominate my body. Each scenario plants another scene in my mind's eye and sends fire coursing through my veins. I'd give anything to spend the rest of my life reenacting every single one of them. I moan, pushing back on him as he thrusts gently into me.

He sighs as his fingers skim across my skin to my clit. With the lightest of touches, he circles the small bundle. I suck in a deep breath, his scent from his shirt invading my senses. I moan and he presses harder.

"I'd explore every carnal thought flitting through your mind. I'd forge a dreamland of sexual fantasies for you. If only..."

Tears spring to my eyes seconds before he pulls out of me, leaving only the tip remaining. My fingers burrow into the sand, scrambling for purchase as he surges into my pussy. He does it again and again until I'm hanging on by a thread. The music around us builds, weaving with my hoarse cries and his ragged breathing, creating a cacophony of sound floating through the air.

My orgasm dangles just out of reach, and I bite the fabric. His fingers press harder as I quiver around his length. He jerks, groaning my name as he comes. I follow him into oblivion, sobbing through the pleasure wracking my body. I bask in the cadence resonating within me. I arch my back as pinpricks of desire pepper my body. He cradles me against him, skimming his hands across my skin.

"Do you hear it? The music we make together?"

I close my eyes, listening to the gradually fading strains. "It's beautiful."

"As are you," he murmurs, placing a kiss on my bare shoulder before slipping from me and standing.

He pulls me up, then scowls at my dress hanging in tatters around my waist. There's no salvaging it. I'm better off just going naked. His jaw ticks and I roll my eyes. He can't be upset with me since he's the one who ripped it in the first place.

When he sighs, I gather up the remnants of the sleeves and cover my chest. Slipping my arms into them, I bite my cheek. I can't lift my hands above my elbows because of the frayed bodice, but I'm committed now. Not with the mocking look he's giving me. It feels like we fall apart the minute we're no longer coming together.

I snort at the thought, smothering it behind my hand. His nostrils flare before I spin around and snatch up the torch. I didn't think it would burn this long, but it's just one more thing I can't explain. My sluggish mind can't process any more. When I face him once more, he's pulling on his pants, his shirt slung over his shoulder.

He stalks toward me, and I awkwardly hold out the torch. He dodges the flames, horror and confusion stamped on his face. I grimace as he snatches it from me. I should not be allowed near fire. I don't know why I grabbed it in the first place. As I stumble back, my heel touches something wet and I yelp.

The next thing I know, I'm in his arms, the torch lying forgotten in the sand at his side. Heat courses through me, but not the kind I'm used to when he's touching me.

I struggle against him, but he tightens his hold on me. "Put me down."

"You stepped in the water. And you're acting peculiar."

"I'm fine. Now please put me down," I wheeze, though I've

stopped trying to wiggle from his grasp. His third leg is poking me in the stomach, and I refuse to acknowledge it.

"You're behaving as if we've just had an awkward sexual encounter for the first time." He grips my chin, forcing my gaze to his.

"I'm not. I didn't want the torch to burn out."

"And yet it was in no danger of such a thing. You do remember my cock has been in your wet cunt multiple times tonight, yes?" He says it with such conviction, a nervous bubble of laughter crawls up my throat.

I press my lips together and my stomach jumps. He merely raises an eyebrow. I don't know how the hell he expects me to respond. Of course I know he's been fucking me from here until Sunday all over this damn theatre. I also know he's pissed because his precious dress got ruined, and he tried to send me away like a harlot who'd performed her duties for the evening.

When the silence becomes too much, I blurt out, "I'm sorry about your dress."

No way in hell am I going to talk about before. Or what happens after this. There's nothing to say. He gave me one night and that was all. I have to be okay with it. Even if my heart aches at the thought of leaving.

My eyes widen when I realize I'm going to end up experiencing that heartbreak every time I play. If he's cursed to the xylophone and I feel that connection—the one resonating so clearly between us—I can't do it. I'll have to leave the symphony. And I doubt I'll be able to find another position as perfect as this one. Subjecting myself to the heartache every day would be a torture I'd never recover from.

"You think I care about the dress? It was made for you, Melody. If I want to rip it from your body, I will. I *did*."

I mutter something incoherent, trying to pull from his grasp one last time. Yet he won't let me go. Finally, I glare at him, still refusing to address the elephant in the room. He glares right back.

"Perhaps you need more incentive to believe me," he growls, digging his fingers into my lower back.

"Your dick isn't a cure-all, you know. You can't just whip it out and expect everything to magically be okay."

My feet hit the ground as he loosens his hold. "I never said it was. The change in your demeanor is disconcerting. I assumed we moved past your distrust."

I don't fully understand what he's saying. The words make sense, but the layer behind them leaves me more confused than when we started the conversation. His cheeks flush and his jaw tics as he stares over my shoulder at the dark, silent lake.

"This is a deep conversation for a one-night stand," I whisper. "You don't owe me anything, but is this just a fetish thing? Tell a woman you're meant to be together, throw in a few parlor tricks, and they fall at your feet?"

"You're the only one I've spoken to in several centuries. I doubt I'd be able to get hard for anyone but you, anyways."

"Oh," I breathe. "Do you think the only thing we're good at is...sleeping together?"

Calling what we're doing "fucking" seems a bit crass. I doubt he'd appreciate the sentiment that goes with it. From the devastation in his eyes, my alternative didn't lend me any points either.

"How many times must I assure you? I claimed you as mine. I've known since you touched the xylophone who you were to me. If I didn't have to let you go, I wouldn't." His words hold such conviction. A pang hits me in the chest, making it hard to breathe.

"I could come back after the next performance."

He shakes his head. "I'd rather you not put your life on hold for me. The world deserves your music."

"They can hear that whenever I play. And then I'd be close to you while you were..." I wave my hand around, gesturing in what I assume is the general direction of the orchestra pit.

"I will not curse you as well, Melody. I refuse."

I inhale sharply, the pain of rejection mingling with acceptance. He may have claimed me as his, but that doesn't mean I'm incapable of making decisions for my own life. If what he says is true, he wouldn't be able to resist me if I stuck around. I can continue to do what I love. He'll sense me there and realize this is better than me giving up everything I know and love. I'll be there when he's trapped. I'll be there when he's flesh and blood. Perhaps one day I'll be there when the curse crumbles under the weight of my commitment.

"Then let's make the most of the time we have left for now," I murmur. "Show me the bell tower."

Chapter Twenty

Xavier

We're not done. We'll never truly be done. But we've run out of time. The tightness in my muscles tells me how close to sunrise we are. I'd give anything to reverse time and relive this night over and over again.

She reaches for the torch, and I grab her elbow, surveying her dress again. She can barely move her arms and she's spilling out of the neckline. Normally, I would welcome such a sight. Her being restricted, though, especially down here, isn't ideal. If she trips, she'll fall flat on her face unless I'm there to catch her.

I sigh before grabbing one of the billowing sleeves. The lace tears and she freezes, her mouth dropping open. A smirk forms on my face and I raise an eyebrow before ripping the fabric completely. A choked noise leaves her, and I repeat the process with her other sleeve.

Her hands fly to her chest, holding the material up, hiding her breasts from me. As if I haven't worshiped them. Seizing the skirts, I glance up at her once before tearing them, too.

"What the hell are you doing?" she cries. "I'm not walking around here naked."

"The only one who would see you is me, but I don't intend

for you to be uncomfortable, Melody." I step back, pointing at the strips hanging around her body. "Take it off."

"What the fuck am I supposed to wear?"

I yank the dress from her hands and force it to her knees. Her hand lands on my shoulder to steady herself, but she's run out of words to protest.

She plants her fists on her hips as I peruse her body, admiring my marks peppering her skin.

"Had your fill?" she snaps when my gaze reaches her face.

"Never."

She clicks her tongue, attempting to hold on to her ire, but it's rapidly draining from her. The glint in her eyes and the smile she's desperately trying to hide tells me all I need to know.

Instead of sinking into her heat again, I grab my shirt and pull it over her head. I didn't even need to unbutton it. The fabric flutters to her shapely thighs. My cock throbs, mourning the loss of such an exquisite sight.

She glances at her feet and sniffs. "I don't have shoes. They slipped off at some point, but I didn't notice."

"You were otherwise occupied."

She yelps as I tip her over my shoulder and wrap my arms around her legs. The shirt barely covers anything now, and a thrill runs through me. I nip at her skin and she yelps again.

"I can fucking walk!"

"And yet you're not. You will make yourself comfortable while I carry you. If you're good, I'll reward you once we're in the bell tower."

She squirms as I make my way around the lake to the hidden exit. My hand lands on her ass, the satisfying sound filling my chest. I graze her flushed skin with my nails, and she shivers.

"Would you stop spanking me?" she huffs even as she squeezes her thighs together.

"If you truly want me to, yes. Though I doubt you actually want me to stop."

I'm careful as I duck through the doorway. As much as I enjoy inflicting a bit of pain on her in the name of pleasure, I'd rather not knock her out. We'd lose what little time we have left. Not to mention, my world would crumble if harm came to her. Taking care of Chad proves that.

She snorts, bringing me back to reality. "What makes you say that?"

I narrow my eyes at her tone, though she can't see me. Her hands grip the waistband of my pants as her stomach bounces on my shoulder.

Symbols flare to life around us, lighting our way through the dark stairwells. I wasn't sure if they would appear again. I wasn't sure they would appear in the first place, merely hoped whatever magic lived within the theatre would respond to her—to us.

"Every time another handprint appears on your ravishingly lovely skin, your pretty little cunt becomes a bit wetter," I say as we reach another landing, and a sound of protest comes from her. "Should I check? What will I find when I bury my fingers in your pussy?"

"The Sahara," she deadpans.

I chuckle, swinging her from my shoulder to her feet. She gasps as her back hits the wall next to us. I gather her wrists in my hand and trap them above her head. She glares at me as my fingers dip under the hemline of my shirt. I brush over her hip, keeping my eyes fixed on hers. When she tips her chin up, daring me onward, I'm lost yet again.

As I nudge her legs apart with my knee, she inhales sharply and my mouth waters. Her nostrils flare and she shakes her head. Ducking my head, I brush my lips against her neck, and she trembles.

"Would you like me to stop?" I murmur, pressing a kiss behind her ear.

"No," she moans, and her hips buck against me.

I skim my palm up the inside of her thigh, then stop. I bite my lip to keep my delight at bay. Her gaze darts away, and I grip her chin as I flatten my hand between her legs.

Her eyes meet mine, light from the symbols reflecting in them. She's a balm to my soul, soothing the jagged edges within. Her essence fills me in a way I'd never thought possible. She's the symphony playing deep within me.

Stepping back, I drop my hands from her body. Her head thumps against the wall, a flush blazing across her cheeks. Her throat bobs as she swallows and my cock throbs painfully hard once more, remembering how exquisite it was to fuck her mouth.

I give her one more second before I throw her over my shoulder again. She doesn't fight it this time, merely wiggles around until she's comfortable. Her nails scrape down my back and along my sides, sending pinpricks of pleasure through me.

I slip through a hidden door, and she buries her face into my back. My chest swells and I shake my head. I slow, then stop before sliding her off my shoulder and into my arms. Cradling her to my chest, I press a kiss to her temple. She blinks up at me, and a smile blooms across her lips.

The staircase to the bell tower is narrow. I'd love to carry her to the top, but it's not possible. She rolls from my arms, landing on her feet before scrambling up. It takes everything in me to keep my hands from dipping under the hem of her shirt. We follow the curve around and around until we reach a wooden ladder propped against the wall.

"It's bolted down. Don't suppose that's a hammer in your pants?" She grins at me, propping her hands on her hips.

"An illusion, Melody. The ladder, that is. You've experienced how real my cock is when it's buried inside you." I climb the rungs and push against the ceiling. The bolt gives easily, revealing a dark space above. "Voilà."

I hop down, then gesture for her to go first. If she slips, I'd rather catch her than have her grab onto my ankle. She peers into the void and grimaces.

"Maybe you should go first. In case there's spiders."

I guide her by the elbow and set her hands on the worn wood. "Up you go. I'm here every sunrise while in this body. No spiders."

"It's really dark," she whispers, but ascends slowly before freezing and glancing down. "Do not fuck with me while I'm on this ladder."

"I would never," I vow, placing my hand over my heart and bowing slightly.

Her bare legs are a tantalizing sight as they pass in front of me. I grip the rungs and pull myself up after her. Glancing up, I watch her pussy peek from between her legs and my mouth waters.

I may have promised her I wouldn't interfere with her while she's climbing, but that doesn't mean I can't lay her out under the bells and enjoy the taste of her pretty little cunt. My cock swells, making it difficult to pull myself through the trapdoor. I manage...barely.

The hot summer air surrounds us, a warm breeze wafting through the arched windows. Melody pads around the belfry, peeking at the bells as she circles back to me. I lower the door and drop it into place. She eyes it warily, giving it a wide berth.

"It's dark up here. Like the city lights can't even touch us," she says, leaning on folded arms on one of the windows to watch the slumbering town below.

I curl my body around hers and rest my chin on her head. "We're quite high."

"Did this place used to be a church or something? I didn't think they put bells at the top of theatres."

"No. Most thought I had gone mad when I expressed the desire to have them installed. They were afraid it would be an affront to...Well, suffice it to say, no one thought it was a good idea. However, I had money and power, and I wasn't above using either—or both. They put the bells here, and we rang them at midday and before closing night."

My muscles tense as the sky lightens. It's imperceptible to someone such as Melody, but I see it. I've spent so long dreading the sunrise, I've become accustomed to the subtle changes. She sighs, eyes fixed on the stars overhead.

"Do they still work?"

"I don't know. I doubt anyone realizes they're still here. Some of these places don't have bells at all. A shame, really." I've been tempted to try them, but I'd worry someone would come to investigate if they started up in the middle of the night.

"I'll ring them for you. I don't know how, but I'll find a way."

I drop a kiss on her neck as I hold her close. She squirms, her ass pressing against my cock, and I groan.

"One would think you'd be tired after our antics." I continue my quest to map her skin with my lips. She tilts her head, giving me more access.

"You got me all hot and bothered. It's your duty to take care of it."

"Hot and bothered?" I murmur.

She snorts, turning her head toward me. "It means I'm horny. You know what that is, right?"

I chuckle and bury my face into her neck. "Having the horn... yes. I know what that is."

"Having the ho—" Her words end in a squeal as I dip my finger between her legs.

Her wetness coats my hand, and I groan again. "All this for me?"

"Do not tease me, Xavier," she says through gritted teeth.

I puff out a laugh, nuzzling her. She whimpers as I circle her clit, though she doesn't need my help at all. Her hand reaches between us and grapples with my pants before I seize her wrist.

"Your desperation is showing, Melody."

She snorts and I can feel her eye roll, though I can't see her face. "As if I care. I know you want to fuck me. That pogo stick poking into my back is proof of that."

My brows pull low, and my grip on her loosens. She spins to face me, and I plant my hands on the sill behind her. My mind flips through the various terms I've heard over the last several decades, trying to place what the hell a pogo stick is. Clearly, she's talking about my cock, but it doesn't make sense. When her palms run over my chest, I'm jolted from my thoughts.

"Are you okay?" she whispers as she cups my cheeks.

I inhale sharply, then exhale as I stare at her. "What is a pogo stick?"

She giggles, the musical tone swirling around me. It eases my muscles and calms my aching heart. Nothing in my life has ever had such an effect on me.

"It's just a toy." She rolls her eyes when I smirk. "Not *that* kind of toy. It has a spring and you jump on it and it bounces...actually, I have no idea how to describe it without it being dirty."

I slide my hand around the back of her neck and run my lips along her jaw. "No, no. Continue explaining this mysterious toy to me. I'd love to hear all the dirty ways it's used."

She guides my forehead to hers. "It's not that kind of toy."

I meld my lips to hers, prodding her with my tongue, and she opens for me. Everything she does has me falling further under her spell. Her tongue dueling with mine. Her citrusy scent invading my nostrils. Her fingers digging into my chest. And those needy whimpers escaping from the back of her throat. All of it envelops me.

Her hands drop to my waistband, and she tugs me closer, then pushes my hips away. My fingers slide into her hair, gripping the strands and tilting her head to deepen the kiss. I'm so absorbed in devouring her, I don't notice what she's done until her hand wraps around the base of my cock. I groan into her mouth as she strokes me.

Ripping my mouth from hers, I gaze down at the sight. She twists as she reaches the tip, and I pull in a shuddering breath. My pants hang around my hips, but I'm too mesmerized by her handling me to deal with it.

I thrust into her hand, biting my lip to keep from coming all over her. I grab the hem of her shirt and tug it over her head. It hangs off her arm and her fingers flex around my length before she lets go, then shakes the fabric off.

I duck my head and capture her nipple with my mouth as she grips me again. Worshiping the tight bud, I plunge into her hand over and over. When I switch to the other, she cries out and her movements stutter to a stop at the base of my cock. I straighten and wrap my arm around her waist before setting her on the windowsill. She tightens her hold on my cock, and I groan.

"Don't look down, Melody. I'm going to fuck you until you scream my name for the whole of the city to hear."

Fear dances in her eyes, but she tugs me closer, then rubs my cock along her wet cunt. The trust she's placing in my hands to keep her safe doesn't feel deserved. My uncertainty bleeds away as she grinds her clit against my tip. A rumble of primal need rolls from my chest and I grab her wrist. When she lets go, I place her hand on the brick next to her hip.

Her fingers dig into the hard stone, and I grimace. "Hold on to me. Wouldn't want you hurting yourself."

She grips my shoulders, wiggling closer to me. I resist the urge to slam into her. This final performance will be a symphonic poem written just for us.

I ease into her drenched cunt, savoring the way she stretches around my cock. The low groan falling from her lips spurs me onward, and I plunge the rest of the way inside before freezing.

Our eyes meet and the connection between us vibrates. Gradually, I pull out, then sink back into her. She trembles in my arms and uses her feet to push my pants down farther. I pause, cocking an eyebrow, and she purses her lips.

"Take them off," she snaps, though her voice is breathless with a tinge of yearning in it.

Her toes hook into the waistband, and she shoves them down more. I chuckle, then slip from her, much to her dismay. I kick off my pants and her legs wind around my waist, pulling me close.

I embed my cock into her once more, gritting my teeth. Her head falls back and I hold her tightly. The windowsill might be wide and there's no way in hell I'll allow her to fall, but I'm starting to question whether this was the best decision.

"Move," she gasps as her back arches.

I surge into her as she clings to me. My mouth skates across her skin until I find her nipple. I nibble on the bud as my hips move, building her closer to the crescendo of ecstasy.

Every time I hit the deepest parts of her, a moan is forced from her. I'd give all that I am to live right here, buried in her cunt as she spasms around my cock. Her nails dig into my shoulders, leaving marks that will fade much too quickly.

"Come for me," I murmur against her flesh.

"Xavier," she keens, her voice ringing through the air.

She cascades into pure euphoria, bliss stamped across her face. The beginnings of the sunrise streak across the sky, purple mixing with a deep pink. They dance along her body, lighting her from the inside out.

I falter, then duck my head into the crook of her neck. I've seen too many dawns breaking over the horizon to enjoy the moment. Not with the implications it carries along its rays.

I thrust into her still-pulsing cunt, drawing out her pleasure as long as possible. I'll coax everything from her body so she'll never forget this night. I'll imprint my existence in her mind so she'll remember this time we had together—for all eternity.

"Give me your everything. All you are. All you'll ever be. Your very essence, little muse," I whisper.

"Yours," she breathes, cradling my cheeks.

Our lips crash together as I detonate. She follows, moaning my name into my mouth. I crush her to me, burying my face in her hair. Still joined, I pick her up and spin around. Sitting isn't easy, but I'm loath to be separated from her. She rolls her hips as she straddles me, peppering kisses along my collarbone.

She settles against me, and I hold her close. I run my fingers through her hair, and she shivers. I close my eyes, and a small smile dances across my lips. The cold from the stone seeps into my back, but it's not enough to fight off the familiar swirl of magic drifting through the air. I swear the sound of the bells ring in my ears, covering whatever lingering strains of the music we've made. It's new and glorious—a testament to what we've created together.

A single strand threads us together as another day dawns. It wavers until settling into a clear single note. The perfect tone personifying our journey to discovering one another. A peace settles over me at the hope encapsulated within the sound. If I hold on tightly enough, nurturing the fresh beginning, perhaps we won't be parted. Perhaps this won't be our end and instead our beginning.

Her sigh echoes around me. "Stay with me, Xavier."

"Forever."

Thank You

Thank you so much for reading Xavier and Melody's story!
Ready for another adventure?
Check out the other works by Emilia Abraham:
emiliaabraham.com

If you'd like to hear about the other stories that have been living in my head, sign up for my newsletter (including extra scenes & a novella), visit my website, or follow me on social media visit: https://linktr.ee/emiliaabraham

Special Thanks:
Emily Renee-Beta Reader
Dragon Smith Publishing-Editor
K.B. Barrett Designs-Cover Designer/Formatter
Krysten & Catlyn-Omega Reader

Other Works

Also by E. Abraham:

Shadows of Synd:

Under the Shadows-Book 1

Between the Shadows: Novella

Running From Shadows-Book 2

Becoming Shadows-Book 3

Shadows Within Us-Book 4

Beyond the Shadows-Book 5

Shadows of Synd Novel: Raised by Shadows

Ruins of Rima:

Spin-off Series

Chasing Darkness-Book 1

Charmed by Darkness-Book 2

Havoc in Harris:

Phantom Betrayal-Book 1

Available on Newsletter:

Extra Scenes
Bridging Epilogues (Shadows of Synd-Book
1 & 2)

Also by Emilia Abraham:

Stuck at Sundown

Write on the Edge

The Cryptid Chronicles:

Bewitched by Bigfoot

Seduced by the Sliver Cat

About the Author

After many years of dreaming of becoming a full-time writer, Emilia Abraham took the leap, bringing her words to print. From sweet contemporary romance to spicy why choose and everything in between, she focuses on the happily ever after.

Emilia lives in the Upper Midwest with her husband (who's probably sick of listening to her expound on fictional men) and three kids (who try to steal her post-it notes). When she's not writing, she enjoys reading, playing video games, and consuming copious amounts of energy drinks.

www.ingramcontent.com/pod-product-compliance
Lightning Source LLC
Chambersburg PA
CBHW020807310726
48969CB00002B/733